Praise for the Hillbilly

Debutante Cafe

"There is nothing like a story told in the voice of a southern author! Kathie Truitt has that southern perspective on everyday life in a small town and is the southern voice of great storytelling."
—**Phyllis Hoffman DePiano**, Southern Lady magazine

"With *Hillbilly Debutante*, Kathie Truitt delightfully opens the curtains to quirky, small-town characters in a way that is reminiscent of a cross between Garrison Keillor and Phillip Gulley. If you grew up in a small town, you will know and love these people. If you didn't, you will love them anyway."
—**Dr. Eddie Randolph**, Harding School of Theology, Memphis, TN

"Such a delightful visit to small-town America with quirky characters and no shortage of intrigue!"
—**Joni George**, author or Old Centennial Farmhouse (oldcentennialfarmhouse.blogspot.com)

"A great 'beach read' with a nice twist at the end...small towns can hold big secrets...and a cast of characters I'd love to see more of."
—**Meredith Kirkpatrick**, jewelry designer (huncamuncadesigns.com)

"The *Hillbilly Debutante Café* is a mixture of 'Fried Green Tomatoes,' 'Steel Magnolias,' and 'Mayberry RFD' with a bit of 'My Name is Earl' sprinkled on top."
—**Rick 'Hutch' Hutchinson**, television producer, Nashville, TN

"Kathie Truitt depicts life in a small town in the most awesome way... *The Hillbilly Debutante Café* is nothing but good, clean fun."
—**The Spectacles Book Club**, Springfield, MO

"Kathie Truitt has an incredible way of writing that simply makes you want to be in El Dorado Springs, Missouri. I found myself researching the mileage between there and my hometown."
—**Lindsay Bowman**, Greens Fork, IN, author of *Jeans Boots Are Made For Talking* (jeansboots.blogspot.com)

The Hillbilly Debutante Cafe

Kathie Truitt

The

Del

1st PERSON —
BIASED
STORYTELLER.
NICE TRY !
ВРОДЕ Н.В. Гоголя.

KATHIE TRUITT

TATE PUBLISHING
AND ENTERPRISES, LLC

Published by Tate Publishing & Enterprises, LLC
127 E. Trade Center Terrace | Mustang, Oklahoma 73064 USA
1.888.361.9473 | www.tatepublishing.com

Tate Publishing is committed to excellence in the publishing industry. The company reflects the philosophy established by the founders, based on Psalm 68:11,
"The Lord gave the word and great was the company of those who published it."

Book design copyright © 2012 by Tate Publishing, LLC. All rights reserved.
Cover & Interior design by Leah LeFlore

Published in the United States of America

ISBN: 978-1-61862-089-7
1. FICTION / Humorous
11.12.19

For
Brenda DeLano
a shelter in a time of storm

Acknowledgments

As always, thank you to my parents, Bill and Lynda Bishop, for a lifetime of love and encouragement.

To my brother, Chuck Bishop, whose one-liners and anecdotes will keep me full of ideas for a lifetime.

To my Facebook friends for their creativity when I had writer's block.

A very, very big thank you to Brad True, the *real* mayor of El Dorado Springs, and Robb Jolly for their consultation regarding the Viet Nam War.

And to my husband, Jay Truitt, who was not only able to help me get Ollie's story on paper but actually wrote most of it himself.

To all the book clubs throughout the country who welcomed me with open arms—Thank you! This book is much lighter than *False Victim*, but I think you'll like it.

Thank you to my cold readers: Michelle Johnson, Carol Nutt, and Angela DeConti.

To my assistant, JQ McMillion, for all she does.

For Dino, Rachael, William, and Sophia for doing what you do best—brightening my world!

A huge thank you to my team at Tate Publishing:

James Branscum, for taking a chance on my very, very rough drafts,

Amanda Reese, my editor, for taking those rough drafts and smoothing out the edges,

Leah LeFlore, who is the *best* graphic designer,

and last but certainly not least,

the Queen and Goddess of PR and Marketing, Traci Jones, who has promoted me to the ends of the earth and booked me there and back again!

And of course my heartfelt love to the people of El Dorado Springs—I hope my readers love you as much as I do!

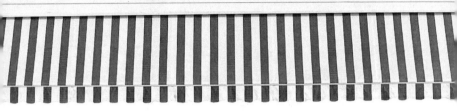

Cast of Characters

MOLLY BERMAN MCCARTY—married to her high school sweetheart, a journalist in Washington, DC. After her husband wins his senate seat, she returns to her hometown, buys a farm, and expects to live a quiet life of happily ever after.

SCOTT MCCARTY—Molly's husband, junior senator from Missouri, easy going, very ambitious, but honest as the day is long. Lives in Washington, DC. during the week and commutes back to Missouri on weekends.

JENNIFER PAPULA—Molly's best friend since kindergarten. Manages Annie's restaurant, but her dream is to find her Prince Charming and leave the confines of small-town rural life.

WALTER SCOTT MCCARTY—known as "Big Scott," Scott's father, originally from West Texas, now the biggest landowner in Southwest Missouri.

KATHRYN MCCARTY—Scott's mother, one of the towns two top social mavens, also hails from Texas, where everything is bigger, including her diamonds, her home, and her hair.

HARRISON BERMAN—Molly's father, owns Berman Ranch, which has been in the family for four generations. Treats Molly like the son he never had and hopes to turn over full operation of the ranch to her when he retires, which probably won't be till he's dead.

WILHELMINA BERMAN—Molly's mother, a former debutante, hails from a wealthy East Coast family, attended the finest boarding and finishing schools. An avid tennis player, horsewoman, and the other half of the town's top social mavens.

WINTHROP JAMES WORTHINGTON III—owner of KESM, the towns radio station, tall, movie-star good looks, oozes charm. His father, WJW II, owned a chain of radio stations throughout the Ozarks, put Winthrop in charge of the El Dorado Springs radio station in hopes of keeping him too busy for womanizing and spending. No such luck.

CONSTANCE WHITE WORTHINGTON—Winthrop's long-suffering wife, was once almost engaged to Michael Dailey before Winthrop rode into town.

ANNE-DONAVAN WORTHINGTON—Winthrop's sister. Very bitter and unhappy, blames her younger brother for the fact that she's a spinster, as she's spent the better part of her life trying to keep him out of trouble and from squandering the family fortune.

MICHAEL DAILEY—temperamental owner of *El Dorado Springs Sun*, his legendary feud with Winthrop dates back to high school when Winthrop "stole" his first true love, Constance White, from him.

PEGGY DAILEY—wife of Michael, and co-owner of the *Sun*. Driven, hard-working, no-nonsense woman, who lives, eats, and breathes the newspaper. Rumor has it that she returned to work eight hours after giving birth to her daughter, Jocelyn, age nine.

"BROTHER JEFF" STEUBEN—young minister, only been in town for about a year. Single, constantly inundated with casseroles and desserts by mothers trying to fix him up with their daughters.

JERRY RAY TURNER—former high school jock, now the town's best mechanic, owns the busiest garage in town. Shocked everyone in town (including his wife) when he came out of the closet as a cross-dresser.

ROLAND THURMAN—fourth generation Cedar Countian, mayor of El Dorado Springs for the past twenty years.

DAVID AND ROSEMARY HUNTER—owners of Serenity Farm until two years ago when they lost their only child Ashley in a riding accident. The couple recently sold the place to Scott and Molly McCarty. The property sits adjacent to Molly's parents' ranch.

OLLIE GRIFFIN—very eccentric character, midsixties, talented musician, lives in and has everything he owns crammed into his 1969 Thunderbird.

ROY BOB BENSON—local ne'er-do-well, is trying to buy the old Hacker's Jewelry building and turn it into a "girly" bar.

"I've often thought that small towns are still a place where those who are different have a niche. Everyone knows them and their shortcomings, accepts them and even looks after them."

— LINDA MYERS, archivist, State of Missouri

Prologue

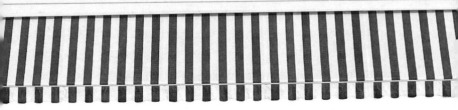

EL DORADO SPRINGS, MISSOURI

There are two very important things you need to know about El Dorado Springs. The first thing isn't the *most* important—but it's still important, nonetheless. It's not that we have the most extraordinarily beautiful park you've ever seen, although we do. It sits in the middle of downtown, right on Main Street, with approximately a five-acre span of green, lush, rolling hills, dotted with park benches, and a gazebo where the oldest city band in the world performs in concert every night, June through August. Nor is it the fact that the foul-smelling spring water that meanders under the ground and gushes out through a spout in the park is known far and wide for its medicinal healing powers.

Nope, the very first thing you need to know about El Dorado Springs, Missouri, population 3,020—now 3,021 since Molly McCarty recently moved back—is how to pronounce it. Boy howdy, if you want to see 3,021 people get downright huffy then just say "Eldo-*RAH*-do" Springs. Yes, I know that's how they say it out west. But how they say it out west is not how we say it *here*. You stick around these parts long enough, and you'll find out that there are a lot of things we do different than most folks. That's not necessarily a bad thing—or a good thing for that matter. It just *is*.

Anyhow, the correct way to pronounce it is "Eldo-*RAY*-do," and usually we just drop the "Springs" altogether. If you want, you can shorten it to "Eldo," which might be a good idea until you get used to saying "RAY" instead of "RAH."

I suppose I'm prejudiced—after all, I did grow up here—but I think El Dorado Springs is the prettiest place in the country. We're nestled in the Ozark hills, less than an hour from the Kansas, Oklahoma, and Arkansas state lines, and the town sits in a T-shape. Highway 54, which runs all the way from Albuquerque to Chicago, comes straight through here and makes the top of the *T*. It's only a two-lane highway, so we don't see too much traffic, usually just city folks turning off on Highway 32 toward Stockton Lake. The long straight line underneath the *T* is Main Street. You can't miss it because there's an arrow-shaped sign pointing north that reads, "El Dorado Springs Business District." At night it blinks on and off.

Go in the direction of that arrow a little ways down the pretty, perfectly tree-lined street, and there sits El Dorado Springs in all of its glory. Well, I suppose nowadays saying "in all of its glory" is stretching it a bit.

Empty storefronts and dusty, lonely sidewalks are pretty near all you see.

It wasn't always like that, though. There was a time, and not all that long ago, either, that a person could buy nearly anything and everything without ever having to go to those big places like Kansas City, Springfield, or Joplin.

Miss Barbara's dress shop carried everything from day clothes to formal dresses, and Hacker's Jewelry was a few doors down. Clemit Casey was the florist and kept busy delivering flowers to the funeral home and hospital, as well as the occasional bouquet husbands would send to their wives for anniversaries or to make up for *forgetting* an anniversary.

Farmers made weekly runs to Jackson's Hardware to find replacement parts and other whatnots, then headed 'round the corner to pick up livestock feed from Producer's Grain before grabbing a quick bite to eat at the Cedar Café. Any time of day, you could find a handful of farmers sitting around a table telling lies or making up corny jokes. My daddy used to say more deals were made sitting at that table over coffee than any other place in the county—even the livestock auction. If it was a really nice late spring or early fall day, you would most likely find those same farmers sitting on the rock wall that surrounds the park.

Doc Reynolds had an office down the street, and you had your pick of two drug stores if you needed medicine. If patients were really sick and in a big hurry to get home, they'd just go to Evan's Rexall, right across the street from Ernie Harris's State Farm Agency. Elton Evans would fill the prescription right fast so they could be on their way.

For those not in so much of a rush, Cooper's Pharmacy, just two doors down, boasted one of the last remaining drug-store soda fountains in the Ozarks. Folks would linger for hours at the long, red Formica-top bar with matching leather-top stools. Mama worked there when she was in high school, and Daddy said she made the best root beer floats this side of the Mississippi.

As a little girl, I loved riding to town with Daddy every Saturday morning to go to the bank. He always used the drive-through, and Mrs. Perkins, the teller, always made a point to slip a sucker through the window with Daddy's deposit slip. She knew me well enough to know my favorite flavor was grape.

But soon—and nobody remembers exactly when—things slowly started to change in our town.

Tri-County State Bank was the first establishment to pack up and move. Rumor had it that bank president Marshall Eubanks had been caught "visiting" Ruby Goode's house during his lunch hour. She lived just around the corner and down the street, and he'd been seen more than once sneaking out her back door when he was supposed to be "in a meeting" or "at lunch."

My aunt Ruthie told Mama that Marshall's wife, Patricia, had given him an ultimatum. He needed to find a job farther away from Ruby's house or she was divorcing him—*but not before taking him straight to the cleaners*. Within the next eleven months, Marshall had convinced the board that the bank would be more profitable up on Highway 54. It definitely made sense, I suppose, due to the traffic on the highway. Anyway, within thirteen months of that, the Tri-County State Bank had a brand-new building directly across the street from Green's Standard Oil Station—less than a block and within perfect viewing distance, I might add, of Marshall and Patricia Eubanks's brick ranch.

Producer's Grain followed suit a few months later and constructed a new facility next to the old Shoe Factory, which had shut down back in 1984. Slowly, over a period of several years, other businesses followed. Some moved farther east and around the corner to Highway 32 where there was a Pizza Hut, Woods Supermarket, Pamida Department Store, and a few other businesses that had never been downtown at all. Evans Rexall moved up to Highway 54, but Orville Cooper decided to just go ahead and close up shop and take his wife, Donna, on a world cruise.

Before long, the only businesses still open were Carl's Gun Shop, the Spring Street Tavern, and the Park Hotel, which really wasn't a hotel at all anymore.

The four-story building, which had been a saloon and hotel back in the late 1800s, had been converted into apartments when Horace and Nanny Longworth purchased the empty building in the 1950s. The couple lived in the—and I use this term *loosely*—"penthouse suite" on the top floor, where every night Horace fell fast asleep in the middle of a smoke.

"You are gonna burn this place to smithereens!" Nanny had scolded him too many nights to count.

And after forty years, it happened. He dozed off during the *Tonight Show*, his Marlboro dangling between his index and middle fingers. Apparently he sneezed in his sleep, and the cigarette went flying across the room, landed in the curtains, and set the whole place ablaze.

It was a miracle that no one was hurt, not even Horace, unless you count a broken heart due to the fact that Nanny up and left him and moved in with her sister over in Walker, a little town just west of here. Although it was only fifteen miles away, Horace never saw Nanny again after that. No matter how much he begged and pleaded with her to take him back, she flat-out refused.

I always thought that was kind of mean of Nanny because, after all, it *was* an accident, and I'll bet you anything that after that he learned his lesson and never, ever smoked another cigarette—at least not before bedtime, anyway. But according to my grandmother, there was a lot more to that story than most of us knew about. Apparently Horace also had a drinking problem, which led to his sleeping-while-smoking habit, which led to the fire that destroyed all they'd ever worked for, not to mention the ninety tenants who were now left homeless. Horace died just two years later, broke, and with a broken heart.

People still do a double take when they drive by that big, vacant spot where the hotel used to be. Funny, it's been over ten years now and it's as if they're noticing for the first time that the big green building is gone. Even though the Parkview Restaurant was built on that same corner a few years back, folks still give directions to "turn left at the Park Hotel."

So now, the Parkview Restaurant, Carl's Gun Shop, and Spring Street Bar are all that's left of a town that used to be hopping every day of the week and so busy on Saturday that sometimes you had to circle around the park at least once to find a parking spot.

Now, even the old rock wall that serves as the park entrance sits lonely with only ghosts of the old codgers that used to linger, day in, day out, spitting tobacco and shooting the breeze.

So yes, looking around right now you might agree that El Dorado Springs, Missouri, pretty much resembles a ghost town, but I can assure you that all that is about to change—which brings me to what I was trying to tell you in the first place—the most important thing about our town. Because, while we might have the prettiest park you've ever seen and spring water that cures just about anything that ails you, make no mistake: the *most important* thing about El Dorado Springs is the people.

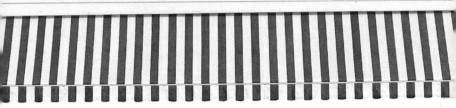

Crazy Is as Crazy Does

ity folks shy away from crazy. When urbanites spot someone that looks even a teens-eensy bit out of the ordinary, they'll cross the street to avoid them. Not us small towners. No, sirree. We love our eccentric characters. The crazier the better, and if we're fortunate enough to have one in our family, then by golly, we wear it like a badge of honor.

I've known more than one normal family that has stretched the truth or outright lied just to stake claim to an odd ball in the gene pool. It's sad when folks have to stoop to that level, but can you blame them? Bless their hearts, they have no stories to recite around the Sunday dinner table or to pass down to the next generation. What the heck could they possibly have to talk about? Probably they just eat in silence or talk about the weather, work, or *worse*—politics.

But not the Griffins. No idle chatter for them over the grits. Their family character was capricious enough to make the best of us green with envy.

There was nothing too peculiar about Ollie other than the fact that he was classically trained in opera. (In a town where Johnny Cash is king, opera is just a tad bit underappreciated.) I also heard he had an extra toe on one of his feet, but I don't know if there's any truth to that—you know how people like to talk and all.

Ollie not only got to play the lead in the school musical all four years of high school, but the summer before senior year he landed one of the lead roles in Benjamin Britten's production of *The Prodigal Son* at the Kansas City opera. By the third night, word of this wonderful new talent spread like wildfire thanks to the raving review in the Kansas City Star. For the duration of the show he performed to a sold-out crowd.

He was invited back the next summer—*without an audition, mind you*—for the lead in *Romeo and Juliet*. But then, just as happened to so many other young men of that era, Uncle Sam called his number and plans abruptly changed.

Sadly, Ollie came back from Viet Nam a very changed young man. Once known for his all-American good looks with piercing-blue eyes, thick, wavy, blond hair, and tan skin, the skeletal soldier that returned home was someone his own parents almost didn't recognize. The gleam in his eyes had been replaced with a vacant stare. His once-buff 185-pound frame had dwindled to 120. His skin had lost its natural bronze tone and now looked ashen.

He became a recluse, shutting himself in his room for days on end, and even when his mama, Betty Sue, tried tempting him with the aroma of his favorite foods,

Ollie still wouldn't budge. His daddy, Earl, had been a veteran of World War II and knew the effects of war on a young man. But even he, as hard as he tried, couldn't get Ollie to communicate.

One day, Ollie informed Betty Sue and Earl that he just needed to be out on his own. Why, his parents were pleased as punch. This was the breakthrough they'd been waiting for. Ollie was ready to rejoin the living.

Imagine their surprise when, instead of buying or renting a house, Ollie bought a slightly used 1969 white T-bird from Bertha Buckles when her husband, Ned, died. Then he drove the car downtown, parked it on the corner of Main and Gay Streets, and moved in. His new house had fewer than 750 miles on it but yet he never, ever drove it, and the only time he ever moved it was when the Park Hotel caught fire. From what I hear, he was parked right next to the building and was forced to move up the street a bit in front of the community center. Once the fire was extinguished and the debris hauled away, he backed it down to its normal spot, and there it stayed for over forty years.

Every year about the time of the first frost, Ollie would climb on his one-speed bike with an empty, red container in his backpack, pedal up to Highway 54 to the Pitt Stop service station, and fill the receptacle with gas so he could start the car and run the heater during the bitter, cold winter nights. His cat, Mo-Ped, slept on the front dashboard, and the few clothes that Ollie had were jammed so tight in the back window that from a distance it looked as if they were vacuum-sealed.

On summer nights he could be found bathing in the city park, and in the wintertime he just didn't bathe at all, which could explain why when he dropped into the Spring Street Tavern for his daily meal, the waitress would seat him in the very back at his own table far removed from the other diners.

Of course, all this just embarrassed Ollie's parents to no end. Earl and Betty Sue pleaded with their son to move back home, but he turned a deaf ear.

Also, when Ollie returned from the war, he never again sang in public—not in church nor with the town orchestra. Many years later, I know for a fact that he received a written invitation to sing at Governor John Ashcroft's inauguration, and he refused that as well, no matter how hard his mama pleaded with him to reconsider.

But sometimes—once in a very blue moon during the first few nights of spring when it wasn't quite warm enough for the air conditioner but just cool enough to leave the windows cracked—folks from a whole block over could hear Ollie's heartbreakingly beautiful baritone, wafting softly throughout the night air.

•

Sugar Jones was born Amariah Pharis Jones. His mama died during childbirth, and his daddy was long gone before he was born, so he was raised by his grandmother.

Eula May Jones, grief-stricken from the sudden loss of her daughter, gathered her new grandson in her arms.

"You are sweet as sugar," she whispered through her tears, kissing his soft, round cheek. From that moment on, he was simply "Sugar." (I don't know if anyone else even knows his given name.)

Anyway, Sugar has this "thing" about numbers. Remember that movie from way back called *Rain Man*? Well, in some ways, Sugar is like Rain Man, but instead of computerizing numeric factors and sums like the character in the movie, Sugar memorizes them. Take the phone book, for instance. Sugar has memorized *every* name all the way from A to Z.

You and I, upon seeing someone we recognize, would say, "Oh look, there goes so and so." Not Sugar. His greeting would be, "Well, hello there, 417-555-1234."

Sugar's specialty wasn't relegated to just phone numbers. He also had this uncanny ability to memorize the birthday of every single person he had ever come in contact with. With that combination, you can be rest assured that no one in El Dorado Springs, Missouri, ever had a birthday without a phone call from Sugar wishing them a happy one.

Numbers weren't Sugar's only oddity, though. He was prone to awful temper tantrums if he didn't get his way, and he often suffered severe bouts of insomnia, which could be a lethal combination, sometimes leading to property damage.

The incident that immediately comes to mind is the time Sugar got angry with his grandmother for not detouring downtown so he could see the Christmas lights.

"I don't have time tonight, darlin'. The Ladies Auxiliary is coming over for our gift exchange." Eula May slipped the keys out of the ignition. She'd had to order her designer cake three weeks in advance from Angie Huckaby, Missouri's award-winning cake designer, who had her own bakery inside the Summer Fresh Grocery. "You sit tight, and I promise tonight I'll make sure you get the first piece of cake."

Six short minutes later, she gently laid the extravagantly decorated looks-too-good-to-eat cake in the back seat. She then situated herself all comfy behind the wheel and by the faint glow of the overhead light saw something that evoked a blood-curdling scream. There in the dash of her brand-spanking-new Ford Taurus was a gaping hole surrounded by a perfect set of teeth marks. Sugar sat there silent as a mouse, staring straight ahead, guilt written all over his face and a big red chunk of dashboard stuck firmly between his clenched teeth.

Yes, we love our eccentric, colorful characters, and we have plenty of them. Ollie and Sugar aren't the only ones by any means, and you'll get to meet the others by and by. I only mention these two first because, although it may seem unlikely, Ollie and Sugar will play key roles in restoring El Dorado to its former splendor.

Now, don't go getting the wrong idea. We're not all crazy. The majority of our folks are normal, hard-working, God-fearing, church-going, red-blooded, all-American folks. And while growing up we tend to daydream about leaving this place and finding fame and fortune, we always end up trying to get back here as fast as we can.

Welcome Home, Molly McCarty

"Thomas Wolfe was wrong." Molly McCarty stretched her slender arms high above her head and inhaled the fresh, honeysuckle-scented air. "You *can* go home again."

It was a perfect end of June morning in the Missouri Ozarks. The soft lowing of cattle and the coo of a distant mourning dove made her smile. This was a stark contrast from the police sirens, honking horns, and city sounds she'd grown accustomed to over the years.

"Who the heck is Thomas Wolfe?" asked Jennifer Papula, a raven-haired beauty and Molly's best friend since third grade. "Oh wait! Wasn't he that new guy that moved here from Little Rock our junior year?"

"No, silly. Thomas Wolfe wrote the classic *You Can't Go Home Again.* Didn't you pay attention to anything at all in Mrs. Wiseman's English literature class?"

Ignoring the question on the grounds it might incriminate her, Jennifer answered, "Oh yeah, Thomas Wolfe…something about bonfires and vanity. I wasn't too crazy about the book. Loved the movie, though. Tom Hanks was in it."

Molly shook her head. "No, you're thinking of *Bonfire of the Vanities* by *Tom* Wolf written in the eighties. *Thomas* Wolfe was a novelist from the early twentieth century. Different person, different book, no movie."

Jennifer just stared at her, not really caring what the heck the differences were between Thomas Wolfe, Tom Wolf, or even Wolfgang Puck, for that matter. Molly, on the other hand, mistook Jenn's stare as interest, so she further elaborated.

"Thomas Wolfe's novel was about a man who writes a book about his hometown. When the townspeople read it and recognize themselves in the plot, they get so angry that they threaten him and warn him to never come back—thus the title *You Can't Go Home Again*. It's a classic."

"And *that* is the prime example of why I've always been known as the 'cute' one and you 'the smart one.'"

Jennifer was right. Not that Molly was bad look-ing—she was cute, with her short pixie-cut blonde hair and big brown eyes with the longest lashes you've ever seen. At five foot one and a hundred pounds soaking wet, Molly had never been one to fuss with makeup or cute clothes. Sure, she had to wear a business suit and fix herself up a bit when she lived in Washington, but as soon as she moved back home, she'd donated all but two of those to the Goodwill store. She would gladly have given those away as well, but as a senator's wife she'd need to look nice every once in a while, and she figured she could rotate the two and folks would be none the wiser. Now her everyday wear consisted of an assortment of t-shirts and jeans or kakis tucked inside Hunter boots.

Jennifer? Now that was a whole other act, altogether! She was what everyone in town considered to be an exotic beauty—tall, with shiny, jet black hair that skimmed past her shoulders and instinctively flipped under, eyes that were just as black and always had a sparkle, almost fiery, like she was always up to no good. Her skin was naturally a dark brown all year round, and at five foot eleven, she looked like an Amazon woman next to Molly.

"Anyway," Jennifer continued. "Is that what you're gonna do while you're sitting in this farmhouse all by your lonesome? Write a book about us?"

"Absolutely not," Molly said flatly. "So yours and everybody else's deep, dark secrets are safe. Besides, all I want to do is stay right here on this farm and become reacquainted with the countryside. If it doesn't have anything to do with cattle or horses, then I'm not interested."

For the life of her, Jennifer couldn't understand why Molly would give up the glamour of the big city to move back to this little podunk town that was barely a dot on the map. Or move into this house, for that matter. She didn't care one bit if the Cape Cod with a wrap-around porch; long, winding, paved driveway with oak trees perfectly lined up and down both sides; complete with a four-stall barn and in-ground pool, looked like it had just jumped off the cover of *Farm and Ranch Living*. This place gave her the creeps.

"You'd be hard pressed to find anything to write about here anyway. I swear this is the most boring place in the universe," she said, trying to ignore the slight shiver that ran down her long, pretty neck.

"Exactly." Molly smiled as she walked down the stairs leading from the kitchen to the back deck onto the pavement. She planted herself next to the pool, dangling her legs in the cool water. Sally, her black lab/husky, trotted through the house out the French doors and plopped down gently beside Molly, laying her head in her mistress's lap. Violet, her white miniature schnauzer, still distressed from the cross-country move, sat under the patio table, too afraid to go near the pool. Finally she lay down and watched Jennifer get up and go to the kitchen, retrieving two Diet Cokes from the refrigerator.

Molly popped the top on the can and took a swig. Jennifer just looked at her with one of her perfectly arched eyebrows cocked. It's that look she gets every time she's about to give you her unsolicited opinion.

"What?" Molly asked.

"Oh, nothing."

Good, thought Molly, taking another drink of her ice-cold soda. She'd taken enough ribbing from her coworkers at the *Washington Post* when she gave notice that she was leaving Washington, DC, to move back here.

Her husband, Scott, had thrown his hat in the political ring as soon as Missouri Senator Kit Bond had announced his retirement. It was a long, nasty, mud-slinging campaign. Scott did win but by a very narrow margin. Votes had to be recounted not once but twice before the winner was called. Interview polls showed that most Missourians felt he had been away from the state too long to fully understand the problems plaguing the citizens. His advisors reasoned that if Molly were to move back to the area full time and he commuted on weekends so everyone could get a good look at him, it would be easier to reclaim that seat during the next election.

Molly needed no further encouragement. She'd felt like she was smothering in that over-hyped, over-crowded den of iniquity that some called The Nation's Capital. She was sick to death of bickering politicians and the constant hustle and bustle, so of course she jumped at the chance to return to her roots. And if doing so happened to help Scott professionally, then who was she to argue? Besides, he'd come to Missouri every weekend, and with the way their schedules had been through the years, weekends were the only time they'd spent together anyway.

She was still mentally patting herself on the back for being such a good, thoughtful wife, when out of nowhere came a thump on the noggin.

"Ouch!" Molly said, instinctively rubbing her head even though it really didn't hurt. "What was that for?"

"For coming back here, that's what for!" Jennifer was disgusted. "Molly, why in the Sam Hill would you give up everything you worked so hard for to come back to this little one-horse town where the most exciting thing that ever happens is the El Dorado Springs Picnic?"

"In case you've forgotten," Molly reminded her, "I never wanted to leave here in the first place. This was Scott's idea. I was sure he'd want to come back here after college. Ranching is ingrained in his DNA as deep as it is in mine, you know."

Molly's daddy, Harrison Berman, was the fourth generation owner of Berman Ranch, a cow-calf operation that sat on 2800 acres of rolling hills just five miles east of town. Scott's family hailed from West Texas, and they'd moved to Missouri before he was even born. Both were only children, and both stood to inherit a lot in land, cattle, and money.

Jennifer was cutting Molly no slack. "Most of us would kill to have a glamorous job and life like you and—"

"Since when is sixteen-hour workdays, a two-and-a-half-hour commute when you live only eight miles away, mixed in with road rage, and the rudest people in North America considered glamorous?"

"Oh, puh-lease," Jennifer argued. "Don't act like your life was all work and no play. Scott's mama is always bragging about the times you two were at White House dinners or attending some big, fancy schmancy gala with some highfalutin Hollywood celebrity."

"Okay, so you got me on that one. I thoroughly enjoyed my time with the president and first lady. Hollywood? Not so much."

"Did you ever get to meet Brad Pitt?" Jennifer asked, temporarily forgetting her disgust.

The only times she'd ever met anyone remotely famous was when hometown girl Sydney Friar won Miss Missouri, but that didn't really count since Jennifer had known her since she was knee-high to a rabbit. The other time was when Senator Bond came through town on a campaign stop to stump for Scott. Afterward they'd all stopped for lunch at Annie's, the diner on Highway 54 where Jennifer worked.

"I saw him at the Kennedy Center Honors," Molly answered nonchalantly as she reached down to pat Sally. "He was sitting at the table behind me, but I never spoke to him."

You could've knocked Jennifer over with a feather. "The sexiest man alive, not to mention a fellow Missourian, and you never even spoke to him?"

"That 'sexiest man alive' thing is a matter of opinion," Molly referred to the title bestowed on the superstar by *People* magazine. "Frankly, I like—"

"Okay, we're getting off subject here." Jennifer held her hand in the halt position. "Remember when we were kids and we'd dream about all the cool places we'd go and things we'd do?"

"No, that was *you* who wanted to leave here for the bright lights, big city. Not me." She'd spent many a night trying to stay awake while Jennifer droned on and on about her hopes and dreams for the future, which did not include Cedar County. It was ironic that Molly was the one to actually leave.

"The main thing I have missed through the years is that sense of community," Molly tried to explain, knowing Jennifer would never understand. "In DC we lived in the same neighborhood for twelve years and never knew our neighbors. People don't exchange pleasantries, let alone have a conversation. Why, a person could be lying on the sidewalk on fire and no one would pee on them to put it out!"

"Okay, so here you are." Jennifer shimmied out of her shorts and tugged at her swimsuit until it completely covered her bottom. "Now what? Scott is still in DC. Why would you want to live halfway across the country from your husband? Who does that?"

"Over half the senators and congress men and women in Washington, that's who."

Jennifer choked on her Diet Coke. "Um…does the name Gary Condit ring a bell? Chip Pickering? John Ensign?"

"That's just mean. Not all politicians are no-good, lying, cheating, scoundrels," Molly argued. "Besides, look at Arnold Schwarzenegger—he lived at home *with* his wife and look at the trouble he got into."

Jennifer pretended not to hear. "And of all the houses for sale in this county, why this one, for cryin' out loud?"

"Number one, it backs up to my dad's land," Molly answered patiently although Jennifer's game of twenty questions was starting to annoy her. "The plan is to cut the fence that divides our property. His cattle will have access to another pond on my land and have another hundred and fifty acres to graze. And number two, I love this place!"

"But somebody *died* in this house," she whispered, as if speaking it out loud would somehow stir up spirits.

"Okay, so someone died in here. Whoop-ti-do!" Molly twirled her finger in the air, then immediately regretted it. "Look, I don't mean to make light of that fact. I feel really bad for David and Rosemary. They're wonderful people, and I know Ashley was their only child. My point is just this: dead people aren't the ones you have to worry about."

"It's just too creepy—especially out here all by yourself."

"My parents are just over on the other side." Molly pointed west through a thick set of trees. "Besides, I've got my trusty sidekicks here." She reached down and wrapped her arms around Sally's neck. The big dog lay on her side and stretched while Molly proceeded to scratch her belly.

"Violet may not be much of a threat," she said as they watched the tiny dog chasing a butterfly, "but Sally is the best watch dog around. Besides, Jenn, it's just like you were saying, this is the most boring place on earth. And I am so ready to be bored."

"After all these years, I'll never understand you, Molly-Moo," Jennifer called her by her childhood name.

"Back at ya, babe!" Molly chided as they high-fived each other. "Now, let's talk about something else! Catch me up on what's been happening while I've been gone. Mama says you're the Queen of All Knowing concerning the goings-on around here. Spill your guts!"

Jennifer swallowed the last drop of her soda. "Well, Ollie Griffin still lives in that same old car—"

"And still bathes buck naked in the downtown fountain, I suppose?"

"Absolutely," Jennifer affirmed. "Do you remember Eula May Jones' grandson, Sugar? He was only about twelve when you left town."

"I think so." Molly tried to picture him. "If he's who I'm thinking of, I used to get phone calls from him every year on my birthday, which I thought was a little weird since I didn't really know him."

"Yep, that's Sugar all right, and don't feel like The Lone Ranger—*everyone* gets a call from Sugar on their birthday. Apparently, as a joke, someone gave him the Kansas City phone book. Well you can imagine Eula May's phone bill the next month. She 'bout tore the house apart looking for that blasted thing! She eventually found it in his room and threw it away, but it was too late. He'd already memorized half of the *As* and in Kansas City that's a lot of names!"

"So what did she end up doing?"

"Well, bless her heart she finally had to have the phone company turn off her long-distance service."

Molly smiled as Jennifer kept talking. Oh, how she had missed this town!

"Anyway", Jennifer continued, "Eula May told Mama that apparently this new medicine that Sugar is on gives him insomnia something horrible and now he's up til all hours, which gives his grandmother fits. He waits til she's sound asleep and he'll leave the house and walk around town all night. She tries to stay awake as long as she can, but you know by midnight she is dead on her feet!"

Molly thought through that for a second and then shrugged. "Well, I guess as long as he doesn't hurt himself, anyone, or anything that's not such a big deal. It's just kind of weird, I guess."

"Trust me, after the Jerry Ray debacle a few years back, everyone around here has definitely tweaked their definition of weird."

"What 'Jerry Ray debacle'?"

Jennifer smiled wickedly, rubbing her hands together as she settled in the Adirondack chair next to the pool.

"You will never believe…"

So engrossed was Molly in the story that she just assumed Sally's ferocious barking and unexpected mad-dash for the paddock was to chase some sort of critter. Neither one noticed the small, slightly built young girl with long, blonde hair wearing a white, eyelet prairie dress leaning against the barn.

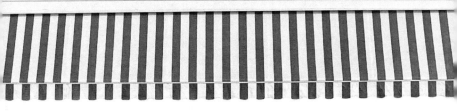

Highfalutin Society

At the precise moment Jennifer was catching Molly up to date on all the area gossip, the newly formed revitalization committee was having their third meeting at the Oaks Steak House, formerly known as the Great Oaks Country Club. The country club had a good run for many years, but honestly, El Dorado folks just are not the type of people to care much about pomp and circumstance. So about a year ago, the last few remaining members decided to close shop and sell the property to businessman Charlie Silvers, and he turned it into what many call the best steak house in the four-state area.

But I digress—back to the revitalization committee. The group had grown from two members to eight, although only seven of them were present. What started out as an idea over coffee after a tennis match between Wilhelmina Berman and Kathryn McCarty, El Dorado's two last remaining society mavens, was soon to take on a life of its own, although they didn't know that just yet.

"I find it very hard to believe there are only eight people in the entire population of El Dorado Springs that care that our town is almost extinct." Wilhelmina, a petite, porcelain-complexioned brunette, had quickly become the leader, although I don't necessarily think she meant to be. She was very prim and proper, always impeccably dressed—I've never seen her in a pair of jeans—and has what Mama calls that "East Coast reserve." Her perfectly coiffed bobbed hair was pulled back in a ponytail at the nape of her neck and secured with a tortoise-shell clip. She's very polite, never says the wrong thing, and has a way of making you think she's in charge without being all puffed up about it.

"And where is Kathryn? She promised she'd be here." Wilhelmina had set the meeting specifically for 11:30 because it was the only time Kathryn could make it. She was slightly annoyed although she was much too classy to let it show.

Just as Wilhelmina was about to call the meeting to order, Kathryn made her usual grand entrance. As much as Wilhelmina was understatedly elegant, Kathryn McCarty was larger-than-life glamorous.

The ladies are best friends, which is a good thing since they're almost related. Wilhelmina's daughter, Molly, is married to Kathryn's son, Walter "Scott" McCarty IV.

Although El Dorado may not have the same kind of "high society" you might see in New York City, or even Kansas City, for that matter, we do have our own version of it—and these two gals are *it*. When Wilhelmina Berman and Kathryn McCarty take up a cause? Well, you're gonna get help whether you want it or not.

Wilhelmina comes from an old, moneyed banking family in Connecticut. Her childhood consisted of English horseback riding, etiquette classes, debutante balls, and fancy boarding schools (she attended Jackie Kennedy's alma mater, the prestigious Miss Porter's School). Although it was expected of Wilhelmina to go to college—preferably an Ivy League school—it was only a formality. Young women of her class were mainly expected to marry well.

Kathryn was from the West, a famous Texas beauty queen before she married Walter "Big Scott" McCarty. She's now in her upper sixties and, like Wilhelmina, still just as fit as a fiddle. She plays tennis, rides horses, and runs five miles every single morning. About three times a year she hops a plane to Dallas to replenish her wardrobe. Her outfits are elaborate and colorful, and while some women would look utterly ridiculous wearing the get-ups she wears, they look absolutely stunning on her statuesque figure. Every day, regardless of where she is going or what she is doing, she makes sure her makeup and hair are done to perfection. Her hair has retained its natural blonde, and a few trips to her plastic surgeon in Dallas has kept her skin almost completely wrinkle free.

While Wilhelmina was always more than happy to slip in someplace unnoticed, Kathryn couldn't just slip in if her life depended on it.

"I'm here! I'm here!" she said in a sing-song voice, making her away across the dining room wearing a bright orange suit with matching hat, handbag, and shoes. A silence came over the lunch crowd as they watched Kathryn glide gracefully to the table where the committee was waiting. She blew air kisses to Wilhelmina and gave a wink and wave to the other members as she situated herself at the table with Peggy Dailey to her left and Peggy's husband, Michael, on her right.

"What did I miss?" Kathryn asked enthusiastically and completely oblivious to the fact that she'd just sat directly between a husband and wife. They both had to scoot their chairs in opposite directions to avoid being hit in the head with her wide-brim straw hat.

"Nothing, dear. I was just complaining that we can't be the only ones in town who care about resurrecting downtown commerce," Wilhelmina's annunciation was always perfect. She always said "going" instead of "goin'" and "talking" instead of "talkin'."

"I've run an announcement in the paper every week for a month now." Peggy sniffed as if someone had just accused her of not doing her part to recruit more volunteers.

She and Michael are the owners of the *El Dorado Springs Sun*, the town newspaper. Since she married Michael twenty-one years ago, she has dedicated every waking moment to that paper. She's never had a vacation, and she even came back to work the day after giving birth to their baby girl nine years ago. Peggy looks pale and frail, but I don't think she's ever been sick a day in her life. Her dirty-dishwater brown hair almost touches her shoulders, and she always keeps it pushed back with a navy blue headband. She has the prettiest aqua-colored eyes I have ever seen and a slight dusting of freckles across the bridge of her nose.

I've always thought if she'd just take a bit of time with herself she'd be quite pretty, but as it stands now, she's plain as day. Mama always said that every woman needs to at least wear lipstick, just to give herself a pick-me-up. And believe me, if any woman ever needed a pick-me-up, it was Peggy Dailey.

"Yes, it's right here on the front page." Michael Dailey picked up last week's paper and pointed to the title in bold font: *Volunteers Needed for City Revitalization Committee.* "Next week I'm going to start mentioning it in my weekly Rock Wall column."

"What about KESM?" Rosemary Hunter asked in a quiet, mousy voice. "I listen all day at work, and I've never heard anyone talking about it on the air. Has anyone submitted an announcement?"

"Pshaw!" Michael bristled at the mention of the radio station. All of a sudden, Peggy sat up straight in her chair, and her eyes darted back and forth between Michael and the rest of the committee.

Michael's face turned beet red.

"I sent Peggy over there to hand-deliver the announcement, and that sorry son of a gun ripped it to shreds and let it fall to the floor then practically pushed her out the door!"

To say that Michael hates Winthrop Worthington, owner of KESM would be a major understatement. And, I might add, the feeling is *very* mutual. Their feud dates back so many years ago that most folks have forgotten by now what started it. Some even think it was just a fight over advertising dollars. El Dorado isn't really big enough to support a newspaper and a radio station, especially now that most of the advertisers have gone out of business. Of course, that competition just fueled the fire between Michael and Winthrop, but that wasn't what started it.

Michael Dailey and Constance White were in love. They were an unlikely pair. She was a beauty queen with thick strawberry blonde hair, cornflower blue eyes, and creamy white skin. Michael was the typical nerd with thick pop-bottle glasses. His dark brown hair was always a mess and his clothes weren't much better. His shirt was usually wrinkled and half untucked. No one ever quite understood the attraction between the two, but nevertheless they'd been almost inseparable all through high school. Throughout their senior year, Michael put in extra hours at his job in the newspaper office to save for an engagement ring. In August, right before college, he'd saved just enough money to purchase the ring he'd seen in the window at Hacker's Jewelry.

He carried that ring in his pocket for two whole weeks just waiting for the perfect moment to pop the question. He was going to suggest they get married over Christmas break. That would give Constance plenty of time to plan a wedding, but they wouldn't have to live apart for very long. He pictured her beautiful smile and the surprise in her twinkling blue eyes when she opened the little gold box and saw the princess-cut diamond sparkling back at her.

But on that bright, moonlit night as Michael and Constance sat on the stairs of the park gazebo, his hand grasped around the little pink box in his pocket, it was he who was surprised. Because while he'd been putting in all those hours at work, he'd been too busy to notice that someone else was moving in on his girl.

•

Winthrop's father, Winthrop James Worthington II, owned almost every radio station throughout the Ozarks—however, none that he trusted his arrogant, flashy, playboy son to take over. Winthrop's radio stations were his babies, so when Winthrop III flunked out of college due to his partying ways, he knew he had to come up with a different plan. At first he'd insisted that the boy go out on his own and make his own way.

"He's been spoiled and coddled for way too long," Winthrop II bellowed to his wife, Anne-Marie. "He needs a lesson on what it's like to have to really work for a living without riding on the coat tails of the family name."

But it was no use. Winthrop III couldn't seem to hold a job for any longer than a month, some not even that long. So when old Mr. Worthington heard about KESM, a radio station of only five hundred watts in a small town just north of Springfield, he did what he had to do. He bought it and handed it over to Winthrop and ordered the boy's sister, Anne-Donavan, to keep an eye on him and "help" him run the place, both knowing full well what that meant. Winthrop would party, and Anne-Donavan would do all the work.

So while Anne-Donavan slaved away seven days a week, Winthrop did what he always did—spent all his time cattin' around town—under the guise of networking, of course, although he didn't fool Anne-Donavan (or anyone else) for one split second.

One day when he peeled his flashy new sports car into Simone's Drive-In for one of their famous hickory burgers, he saw the prettiest girl he'd ever seen in all of his twenty-one years. Why, she looked like Grace Kelly on roller skates.

He didn't care one iota that she was practically betrothed to another. He saw what he wanted, pursued it, and, like everything else in his life, got it. They were married by Christmas.

So, after college Michael "settled" for Peggy, a girl he'd dated on and off (and who was head over heels in love with him) his senior year at Missouri State. They both worked for a few years at the *Springfield News-Leader*, and when John Smith, owner of the *El Dorado Springs Sun*, put out word that he wanted to sell the paper and retire, the couple jumped at the opportunity.

To this day Michael and Winthrop still despise one another. Getting Michael's okay for Peggy to go down to the station and ask Winthrop to run the ad took some talking, and when Michael finally gave her the okay, Winthrop tore up the announcement! When he heard what had happened, Michael had been ready to march down to the station himself and teach Winthrop a lesson. But Peggy stopped him, reminding him that he'd be playing right into Winthrop's hands. After all, there's nothing that cad Worthington would like more than to have an excuse to have Michael arrested.

Wilhelmina sighed. "I'll go over and have a talk with Winthrop. He is difficult to deal with, but we do need the extra publicity."

"Difficult? That's the understatement of the decade. Why, he's a no-good, snake in the grass—"

Mayor Roland Thurman cut Michael off before he could go off on one of his tirades on the character of Winthrop Worthington III. "Let me see if I can get some of my councilmen to join. That'll add at least four more to the group."

"And I'll see if I can't talk a few of my members into joining," Jeff Steuben piped in. "Brother Jeff," as he's known by everyone in town, is the minister at the Church of Christ over by the hospital. If I was guessing, I'd say he's about thirty years old. He's over six feet tall and looks an awful lot like that heartthrob actor Patrick Dempsey! An *unmarried* Patrick Dempsey, I might add. Church membership skyrocketed when he came to town about a year ago—especially among young single women within a fifteen-mile radius.

"That would be wonderful." Wilhelmina smiled, knowing she could most likely expect a surge of young, single, female volunteers. She then looked across the table at Roland, about to take a bite of the fried chicken the waitress had just put in front of him. "Mayor, I am really counting on you being able to coax your councilman into joining us—maybe even the city manager. It will just make us that more credible when we start applying for state and federal grants.

"And, Kathryn, we need to sit down and brainstorm, come up with a plan on how we can persuade more of our citizens to get involved. All of these ideas are useless if we don't have enough people on the committee."

"Well, darlin', we need to do something pretty darn quick." Kathryn's all-out Texas drawl stands out, even here in Southern Missouri; it's slow as molasses and soothing as a kitten's purr.

"Jennifer Papula told me that Bobby Joe Allen is fixin' to paint the Spring Street Bar in Kansas City Chiefs 'red and gold.'"

"I don't know why he'd want to go and do that." Ernie Harris had kept quiet till now, just taking it all in, trying to see exactly what this revitalization committee was all about. "It's not like they've had a winning season in the past decade. He'd be better off to paint it up in black and gold for Missouri Tigers."

Wilhelmina cringed. It would be just like Bobby Joe to do it, too. Back in 1976 during the country's bicentennial, he had painted the building in red, white, and blue stripes with fifty stars all bunched up together over the left-hand side. Tacky, tacky, tacky. About six months ago he'd repainted the building a very tasteful beige color, and if Wilhelmina and the committee had their way, beige it would stay.

They were in the process of lobbying the city government to put provisions into place that would restrict how business owners painted and decorated the outside of their buildings.

Wilhelmina knew the importance of portraying a good image to lure prospective businesses to town. What she didn't know was that soon enough Bobby Joe's psychedelic paint preferences would be the least of her worries.

You've Gotta Show Me

You know that old saying "you gotta see it to believe it"? Or "the proof is in the pudding"? Well, Missouri isn't called the "Show-Me State" for nothing. And Molly, being a true blue, born-and-bred Missouri girl, had to see it for herself—"it" being Jerry Ray Turner.

Molly wasn't the least bit surprised when Jennifer told her that Jerry Ray forfeited his college football scholarship to stay home and open up his own auto mechanic shop. After all, lots of kids 'round here skip college and go straight to work. And if the truth be told, as good as Jerry Ray was at sports, he was destined to make a lot more money fixing cars and farm equipment than most near anything else he could get a degree in—provided he didn't want to be some bigwig brain surgeon or—*God forbid*—a lawyer!

No, none of that surprised Molly. But surprise couldn't even begin to describe what she felt when Jennifer revealed that Jerry Ray Turner—all six feet two inches of him—had taken a shine to women's clothing.

"Shut up!" Molly's mouth gaped open in mock horror. "You're telling me that Jerry Ray—*our Jerry Ray*—

is a cross-dresser?" As hard as she tried to conjure up the likeness of big, tough Jerry Ray in a dress, it just kept being pushed away by the image of him in shoulder pads and a helmet.

"You mean to tell me your mama, nor Scott's, has ever kept you up to date on the shenanigans that go on around here?" Jennifer asked, secretly pleased that she had been the privileged one who got to clue Molly in on the biggest scandal in the town's history. Or at least as far back as this generation could remember.

"No," Molly answered, eyes shut tight, the image of Jerry Ray in heels, pearls, lipstick, and mascara refusing to surface. "About the only thing they've filled me in on over the past twelve years is who all is having babies, only because that's their own little unique way of telling me to get a move on it."

"Well…" Jennifer leaned in closer. "You remember Tracy Green from Stockton, don't you? The one with all those brothers and sisters? I think there were nineteen or twenty kids in that family. Can you imagine? Twenty kids? Lord, have mercy! Anyway, Jerry Ray was married to her for about four or five years. Wanda Rogers at the diner told me that Becky Brown told her that Tracy came home from her teaching job one day and found him all decked out in her jewelry! Can you imagine that? Comin' home and findin' your very own husband with silver bracelets dangling from both arms and rhinestone clip-ons dripping from both ears?"

Actually, Molly couldn't picture Scott any more than she could Jerry Ray.

"So, anyway he brushed if off, telling her that he was just playing around in her jewelry box tryin' to get an idea of what she did or didn't have and what he needed to buy to add to her collection. Their anniversary was in a few weeks, so it made perfect sense and she didn't think anything else about it.

"*Until...*" Jennifer stopped just long enough to take a breath. "She snuck in early one night and caught him standing in the kitchen, frying himself up a baloney sandwich wearing her red bra, red panties, and red matching robe draped across his shoulders in *full-face makeup.*

I guess he got caught *red-handed.*" She giggled at her own joke. "So at that point he had no choice but to fess up. Tracy went out the very next day and filed for divorce. That's when he decided to just go on and jump out of the closet."

"You mean 'come out of the closet,'" Molly corrected.

"No, honey, he pretty much took a flyin' leap. On Wednesday he was the same old Jerry Ray we know and love, and next mornin'? Bingo! He looked like an overgrown, hairy cocktail waitress."

•

Overgrown, hairy cocktail waitress, indeed, Molly thought as she sat in front of what used to be known as Green's Standard Oil Station but was now Turner's Garage. Jerry Ray had purchased the building when Leo Green decided to retire, exactly six weeks before his and Tracy's wedding.

Now here he was with his head underneath the hood of a Ford F-150 pickup, long blond locks cascading down the middle of his broad shoulders, held in place at the base of his neck by, *of all things,* a pink barrette.

Last time Molly had seen him, he'd had his same old crew cut, wearing a pair of tight, worn-out wranglers, snug t-shirt that accentuated his buff arms, and an old pair of steel-toed work boots.

What a contrast in a pink rhinestone-studded tank top tucked in to the waist of a pair of skinny jeans and a wide leather belt slung low across his narrow hips. On his size thirteen feet were a pair of pink Jack Rogers sandals, his giant-sized, masculine toenails painted the same neon pink as his top.

Molly's thoughts were all jumbled up. First, *This is weird on so many levels;* to, *I had no clue they made shoes that big;* and finally, *Why is he so dressed up when he has a job fixing cars?*

Jerry Ray heard the engine of Molly's 1952 barn-red Chevy pickup cut off and a car door slam.

"I'll be with ya in just a sec." He reached across the fender of the vehicle for a hand towel and wiped his large, perfectly manicured hands. Molly self-consciously glanced down at her own neglected nails.

She stood there quiet as a church mouse suddenly nervous and wishing she hadn't let her curiosity get the best of her.

Now before I go any further, there is one thing you need to know. Do not go picturing someone like Ru Paul or some of those other cross-dressers you see on TV. You know what I'm talking about—the ones that are so gorgeous they make you want to go out and get a makeover and go shopping. Well, I'm here to tell you right now, there was absolutely nothing feminine or beautiful about Jerry Ray Turner. He simply looked exactly like what he was—a big brut of a man wearing lipstick and chest hairs poking out between his pearls.

As he turned to face her, Molly said a quick prayer. *Lord, please do not let me laugh.*

She no sooner got that prayer sent up to the Lord himself when Jerry Ray turned around. When he saw it was Molly, one of his best friends that he hadn't seen since before you-know-when, he quickly sent up a prayer of his own. *Lord, please do not let her laugh.*

God must have been listening, because the next thing you know they were hugging and doing air kisses so Jerry Ray wouldn't smear his lipstick.

"Well, slap the dog and spit on the fire! Molly Berman McCarty. I have not seen you in a coon's age!"

He held her at arm's length and took a good long look at her.

"Why, you have not changed one bit!" he declared.

"Neither have you!" The words just slipped out— like an automatic response when someone asks "how are you" and you reply "just dandy" even though your whole world might be crumbling around you.

"I-I mean, you, um…you look, *younger…better.*"

Better? What a stupid thing to say! Quick! Think of something! Her face was as red as the stop sign on the corner.

"I heard you were back in town!" Jerry picked it back up, pretending not to notice the proverbial eight hundred-pound gorilla between them. He nodded over Molly's shoulder to the old pickup. "And still drivin' ol' Dixie, I see."

Sally was sitting in the front passenger's seat, and for a moment he thought it was a person.

"As a matter of fact, that's why I'm here," Molly lied. Well, it wasn't a complete lie. Her daddy did tell her when he turned the keys over to her that the truck was due for a tune up.

"I was hoping you could maybe fit me in sometime in the next few days. Dixie will be my main set of wheels, and I want to make sure she gets a quick once-over before I start driving all over kingdom come."

"There is never a wait for the Berman family." He went inside, motioning for her to follow him as he penciled her name in the appointment book. "For you, I even make house calls."

And that was the truth. Jerry Ray would have roped the moon for anyone related to the Berman family. If it hadn't been for Harrison, Jerry Ray would have been forced to close his shop doors a long time ago.

You see, Jerry Ray had the wise idea to choose the town celebration, otherwise known as the Founders Day Picnic as his coming-out party.

El Dorado Springs is a place that sits right smack dab in the middle of the Bible belt and doesn't look too keenly on misfits like him. Oh, sure, they'll embrace folks like Ollie and Sugar, and they don't even mind Johnny Tate, the old guy who sits in Annie's Drive-In sipping a cup of coffee and eating napkins. But this is a place where they worship high school football on

Friday nights and Jesus on Sunday mornings. So when a full-grown man—an athlete at that—overnight starts dressing like a woman, well, that was just too much for folks to handle.

It's not like he'd expected people to roll out the red carpet, so the mock wolf-whistles and rude remarks didn't faze Jerry Ray a bit. He could even tolerate the occasional middle-of-the-night drive-by and flinging of rotten eggs or tomatoes at his house. No, Jerry Ray thought he was ready for the way his life was about to change, but in actual fact, he had no idea just how much it would.

Business came to a screeching halt. Immediately customers flocked to his garage like bees to honey demanding the keys to their vehicles, even the few that had to hire a wrecker to transport theirs to a "normal" mechanic. One who wasn't a pervert—a deviant.

But not Harrison. Every week he'd bring in one of his vehicles for an oil-change or tire rotation, with Jerry Ray knowing full well that he was just doing it to be kind. Once Harrison's pickup truck had tires rotated, new brake pads (his old ones were fine), and an early oil change, and Wilhelmina's Cadillac had gone through the same routine, Harrison would have his foreman bring in one of the feed trucks, followed by the cattle truck until the whole process started all over.

Jerry Ray's whole existence for the next five months was supported by Harrison and Wilhelmina Berman. He couldn't prove it, but he was sure they'd had a pow-wow with Big Scott and Kathryn McCarty, because the next thing you know he was servicing Kathryn's Range

Rover and fixed a tractor tire brought in on the back of the flat bed by one of the hired hands.

By Christmas of that year, one by one, his regulars started trickling back. Now, three and a half long years later, business was once again booming.

"How about eight o'clock tomorrow morning?" Jerry Ray asked, pencil poised.

"I'll be here," Molly promised, hoping that maybe her mama or daddy could pick her up.

"You can always borrow the Tweety Bird if you need to." Without looking up from the appointment ledger, he nodded to a yellow 1960 Corsair.

Molly's blue eyes got as round as saucers. Half of Cedar County would sell their grandmother to drive that car.

"Really? You'd *really* let me drive it?" She clapped her hands and jumped up and down like a silly schoolgirl taking her daddy's car out for the first time.

Jerry Ray smiled, and for a moment she saw the same sparkle in his eyes that even metallic blue shadow and Tammy Faye Bakker false lashes couldn't disguise.

"Only you, Molly-Moo. But don't tell Jennifer. She's been buggin' me to let her drive it, and considerin' the fact that she's had two fender-benders already this year, there ain't a snowball's chance in Hades of that happenin'."

"It's our secret," Molly agreed, both of them knowing that as soon as she drove it off the lot it would be all over town within fifteen minutes.

He watched her as she walked away, got behind the wheel of old Dixie, and pulled off onto Highway 54,

Sally's head out the passenger's side window, tongue flailing in the wind.

Hmmm, he thought, heading back to the Ford truck he'd been working on earlier. *Just a bit of lipstick and mascara, and that Molly McCarty could be such a beauty.*

Peggy Dailey, Reporter Extraordinaire —Almost

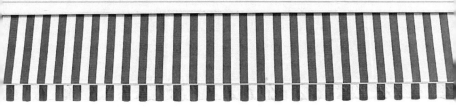

While most little girls played dolls growing up, Peggy Dailey spent her childhood pretending she was Barbara Walters. From the time she was nine years old, she had her life all planned out. She would graduate from Drury College in Springfield with honors, stick around, work for one of the television stations, learn the ropes, and then when her reputation was firmly planted as a journalist, she would pick up stakes and head out to New York City.

But as you know, plans are meant to change. Instead of the Big Apple, here she was in the Walnut Capital—married to a man who tolerated her at best- and where the biggest thing that usually happens was Friday night football. *Usually.*

Case in point: Robert Oglesbee was the first person on death row to be executed in the state of Missouri since the 1940s. His arrest and conviction in the deaths of nine women in the southeast part of the state (known as the bootheel) earned him the nickname "the Bootheel Butcher."

Anyway, news trucks, cameras, and reporters from all major networks camped outside the corrections center, which was in Jefferson City at the time. A group of almost 150 protesting the death penalty held a candlelight vigil, sang "Amazing Grace," and held up signs demanding then-governor John Ashcroft pardon Oglesbee. He refused.

What does all of this have to do with Peggy and El Dorado Springs? Well, it's state protocol to send an executed prisoner's body back to the county of birth. For Robert Oglesbee, that was Cedar County. Bryce Dustman, an old college chum of Michael's, gave him the heads-up that Oglesbee's body was on its way, although he didn't know which cemetery.

"There are fifteen graveyards from here to Stockton," Peggy whined when Michael instructed her on her new assignment. "Not to mention those little out-of-the-way burial plots stuck off in the boondocks that nobody knows about."

"Then you better get started. There's a snowstorm on the way," he replied, not bothering to look up from his computer.

Four muddy, gray cemeteries later, a light mist began to fill the air. It was 4:45 and would be getting dark soon. Love Cemetery, five miles east of town with not a house in sight, was definitely the last place Peggy wanted to be. Buttoning up and popping the collar on the old, blue wool coat she'd had since high school, which was too many years ago to count, she made her way toward the cemetery gate.

Spotting two groundskeepers in the distance—a man and woman—she felt a sense of relief that she wasn't alone. The two were so engrossed in their work that even with the echo of the car door slamming shut they still didn't acknowledge Peggy's presence.

"Yoo-hoo." Peggy waved, and the woman stopped and made eye contact with Peggy for a split second, but she was expressionless and she didn't speak. Something in her eyes gave Peggy the creeps, but she quickly brushed it away. After all, being in a country cemetery far away from civilization when it's near dark tends to wreak havoc on the imagination. "I'm Peggy Dailey with the *El Dorado Springs Sun*. Can you tell me if Robert Oglesbee is being buried here?"

"Never heard the name before," was the woman's abrupt answer before turning her attention back to the grave she was tending. All clichés about graveyards at dusk set aside, both of these folks were scary as all get out. They were eery-enough looking from a distance, but as she got closer, it only got worse—especially the woman. From the top of her head to above the ears, she had blonde roots. The rest of her hair was pitch-black, giving the appearance of being bald on top and that her hairline began at her ears and grew downwards, just skimming her bony, sweater-clad shoulders. Add the spindly hands and deep crevices etched in her face, and she looked exactly like a witch.

The old man, wearing a St. Louis Cardinals cap and dressed in overalls over a red flannel shirt, flashed

Peggy a toothless grin and tipped his hat but didn't say a word. He did, however, start having a coughing fit—one of those gross, loose, phlegmy kinds that makes you almost sick at your stomach when you hear it. Then after sloshing it around in his mouth, he spit a big loogie in Peggy's direction, narrowly missing her loafer-clad foot.

She started to fuss at the old man to watch where he was aiming, but when she did her little two-step to dodge the spitball, she caught sight of the small, silver, temporary grave-marker that funeral homes use until the permanent tombstone can be set.

And there it was, plain as day: Robert Dean Oglesbee.

"Here he is!" Peggy exclaimed, forgetting her annoyance at almost being spat upon. "I hope I can get a good picture in this light, I might have to use a flash…"

She was giddy as she fumbled for the camera case. This was going to be a *big* story. "Newspaper Reporter Finds Bootheel Butcher's Grave" would be the headline, and of course her picture would be plastered for all to see. And Michael—yes, Michael—oh, how proud he would be! Her fantasy of him embracing her and dipping her for a passionate kiss was abruptly squelched by the thud of two shovels being jammed into an upright position into the ground. What Peggy saw next sent a cold chill down her spine that had nothing to do with the drop in temperature or the heavy snow that had begun to fall.

The man and woman weren't groundskeepers. They weren't even grave *diggers*! They were grave digger-*uppers*! That's right! Less than twenty-four hours after

Robert Oglesbee was put six feet under, these two were digging him up.

Peggy looked down at the pile of fresh dirt. They were a quarter of the way finished! How did she not notice? The old man started screaming something about being Oglesbee's father, and the woman, who Peggy then naturally presumed was Oglesbee's mother but later found out was his wife, swiped at and successfully grabbed Peggy's camera and then went for Peggy. Later she would find out that the man and woman had exhumation papers and were in their legal right to move Oglesbee's body to a final resting place, but right this moment Peggy had no way of knowing this, and all she could picture was her own dead carcass being buried in this mad man's grave and no one ever finding her.

This is definitely not the way I expected to die! She broke away and ran for dear life back to her car, not even remotely aware that she'd lost a shoe during her mad dash to safety.

The whole bizarre incident received a small mention on the ten o'clock evening news on all the Springfield and Joplin television stations, but there was no mention of the reporter who had stumbled (literally) upon it. And there was only a small byline on the front of the *El Dorado Springs Sun*, which gave no mention of her name, only calling her a "local female reporter."

"Everyone knows you're the only female reporter I have, so there was no need to mention your name," was Michael's excuse when she asked him why he'd not given her credit.

Good grief, she thought. *I can't even make my own paper.*

Through the years, there had been plenty of "almosts" for Peggy. But every story she chased seemed to be a dead end.

Take the past few weeks, for instance. It was unusual for the school board to call an emergency meeting during the summer, and because of this, Michael knew something was up.

"Rumor has it they're getting rid of Coach Deane. Now why would they fire a coach who's had a four-year winning streak? As a matter of fact, he's the winningest coach in the school history. Find out what's going on," Michael ordered Peggy. Then with a smarmy grin, he added, "I'll bet you this newspaper office he had something going on with the cheerleading coach. Or maybe it was that cute new art teacher. Either way, it had to be something along those lines. You just don't fire a winning coach for no reason."

As it stood, there was no scandal with the cheerleading coach, art teacher, or anyone else. All Peggy found in her research was that the coach was the victim of a handful of parents pitching a hissy fit because their boys didn't get the field time Mommy and Daddy thought they deserved. No real story, just a dead end—much like her career and her marriage to Michael.

Speaking of Michael, she wished she'd taken him up on that bet after all, because as the new owner of the *El Dorado Springs Sun* the first thing she would do is kick his sorry behind to the curb. She imagined selling the paper to the highest bidder and fancied the thought of watching this one-horse town getting smaller and smaller in her rearview mirror. At that thought, Peggy did something she hadn't done in a very, very long time. She smiled.

Pretty Is as Pretty Does

Constance Worthington is just ugly. There. I said it! Mama always told me if I can't say anything nice then I shouldn't say anything at all. But she also taught me to speak the truth, and the truth is she's just an ugly, nasty person—Constance, that is; not Mama.

Now, don't get me wrong—as far as looks go, Constance *is* beautiful. She's a former Miss Cedar County, making it all the way to the top ten at the Miss Missouri pageant her senior year of high school. It's what goes on inside that head of hers that I just don't get. Why, she'd just as soon go out of her way to be evil and spiteful when most of the time it would be just as easy to be nice.

She wasn't always like that, though. As a little girl growing up, even into her early teen years, Constance was a free-spirited, precocious child. Sure, she had a weird fondness for anything that sparkled, but I'm sure that was due to the fact that her mama, Annabelle, entered her in every beauty pageant this side of the Mississippi. Constance was everything from Baby Miss Missouri to the Pork Princess and Beef Queen before winning Miss Cedar County at seventeen.

Of course, Constance was aware of her beauty. I mean, who wouldn't be with a room stuffed full of tiaras, sashes, and trophies? But as far as I know, she never used that beauty to manipulate—until she met Winthrop.

In a world of cowboys, pickup trucks, and Wrangler jeans, Winthrop definitely stood out in his racy sports car, money, and preppy clothes. In a town where dreams are financed by sweat and hard work, Winthrop was used to getting whatever he wanted with nothing more than a flash of his pretty-boy smile. And Constance had fallen victim to his charms.

It only took about seven days for her to realize marrying Winthrop had been the biggest mistake of her life. Maybe it was the constant flirting with other women on the cruise ship during the honeymoon. Or the late nights he kept when they got back and the lame excuses he gave about where he'd been, not to mention the out-of-town trips and the whispers she heard around town about other women. Worse yet was the whispering about *her*, the idea that she'd brought this humiliation on herself. And even worse than *that* was remembering that in a moment of weakness she'd let some forked-tongue fool dangling diamonds and empty promises come between her and the love of her life.

So many times she'd wanted to call Michael and beg him to take her back, but something always stopped her. Pride, I suppose. He didn't marry for a long time, and I've often wondered myself if he would have forgiven all and taken her back. My instincts say he probably would have, but that's neither here nor there. You can't unring a bell.

When Michael did finally get married, Constance took great delight in the fact that the girl he'd brought back to El Dorado was plain as day. This was a pivotal moment in Constance's life. Overnight she went from a beautiful, blonde, modestly dressed hometown girl to a seductively clad, cleavage-baring, flaming red-headed vixen.

Suddenly she was parading up and down, all-around town showing off like a two-bit porn star. Winthrop took sadistic glee in the newly gained attention bestowed upon his wife. His narcissistic ego led him to believe that every man wanted her and she was just another possession he owned that they couldn't have. And although he wasn't about to change his selfish, skirt-chasing ways, he took delight in the fact that Constance must have decided to step up to the plate and be worthy of him.

If the idiot would have taken a moment to pay less attention to other men's wives and more to his own, he'd have seen what everyone else with two eyes saw: that Constance's new image wasn't for *his* benefit at all but a bid to get Michael back. Or at least to make him sorry that he hadn't fought to keep her.

Constance made a career out of slinking her way into the presence of Michael or Peggy at every possible opportunity. She *loved* making Peggy squirm, and she was very, very good at it.

But everyone has a breaking point. For some that breaking point is painfully obvious. For others, it's so subtle that when it happens no one sees it coming until it's too late to do anything about it—which just happens to be the category Constance finally pushed Peggy to the brink of.

The night started out calm enough. It was a typical Wednesday night before church, and Michael, Peggy, and their daughter, Jocelyn, were seated at the Rusty Jug restaurant just like every Wednesday since the place had opened for business three years before. Not coincidentally, in marched Winthrop and his daughter, Victoria, taking the next available table, which, lo and behold, happened to be the adjacent one to the Dailey's. At that point, everyone was playing nice, or at least pretending the other didn't exist. All that changed when Constance made her planned-to-the-second grand entrance and sashayed in front of an obviously appreciative Michael and winked at him. Before taking her seat, she gave an "I dare you to do something about it" smirk to Peggy.

Winthrop didn't see the wink but did catch Michael looking his wife up and down.

"You pervert! Stop ogling my wife." Then he looked at little Jocelyn and said, "What does it feel like to have a loser for a father?"

Without hesitation, the nine-year-old looked him straight in the eye and said, "I don't know. Let me ask your daughter. Victoria, what's it like to have a loser for a father?"

Winthrop's face turned as red as his fancy sports car while Michael roared with laughter. Peggy stiffened, and Constance's sneer became a grim line as Winthrop stood up with enough force that his chair fell backward with a bang. Suddenly, the Rusty Jug got as quiet as a whore in church when the preacher asks if anyone needs to repent.

"You need to teach that brat of yours some manners!" Winthrop bellowed.

Fast as lightning, Michael was out of his chair and standing nose to nose with Winthrop, both screaming and hollering.

Being familiar with Michael and Winthrop and their volatile relationship, and sensing that punches were about to be thrown, Todd Leonard, owner of the Rusty Jug, made a huge production out of introducing his brand-new dessert, walnut key lime tarts.

"You boys have a seat and be the first try the cook's new dessert," Todd insisted, pushing a metal cart filled with fifty teeny, tiny pies.

Less than sixty seconds later, Winthrop was his same old narcissistic self, making goo-goo eyes at Michelle, Todd's wife, not noticing that Michael and Constance were still sneaking looks at each other.

Peggy, on the other hand, had just hit that subtle breaking point I mentioned earlier. She stuck her fork in the dessert, popped it in her mouth, and at that precise moment made a decision that would change her life.

Things That Go Creak in the Night

"Ugh! I'd forgotten how nasty the water smells!" Molly slammed the laundry room door shut, but it didn't do a lick of good—in a matter of seconds the whole main floor reeked of rotten eggs or ten grown men farting; take your pick.

She'd also forgotten about the gritty, sulphury taste and the diamond-sized minerals that settled to the bottom of the drinking glass after a few minutes (which to me looks like something sitting at the bottom of Daddy's toolbox).

Even Violet refused to drink it.

"Don't worry, girl. It's perfectly harmless. I grew up on this, and we'll be used to it in no time." But after a day and a half Molly was afraid the little dog would dehydrate, so she gave in, drove to Woods Supermarket, and bought a case of Ozarks True Country Spring Water.

Violet lapped it up as fast as Molly could pour it in her bowl.

"You are definitely a city dog, aren't you, baby?" She reached down and scratched Violet between the ears. Then she turned to Sally. "You, on the other hand, don't give two ca-hoots about the water, do you?"

Sally quickly jumped up from a lying position and lifted her head. Her soft, expressive, brown eyes that gazed straight into Molly's exuded nothing but pure adoration. Molly cupped the large dog's face in her hands and massaged her scalp and behind her ears.

"There are just too many squirrels and rabbits to chase for you to worry about how the water tastes or smells. Water is just water. Liquid to keep a good dog hydrated, huh?"

Sally's bushy tail thumped the floor as she gave Molly a wet lick on the kisser. "And you are a good dog, aren't you, girl?"

Thump, thump, thump.

"Yes you are!"

Jealous that Sally might be getting all the attention, Violet wormed her way in between. The next thing you know, Molly was rolling around on the kitchen floor with both dogs.

"You're my babies!" she said, snuggling one dog in each arm. Molly always talked to them like they were human, almost as if she expected them to talk back to her. And it wasn't for their lack of trying, either—at least on Sally's part.

You see, there was something that bothered Sally tremendously. Several times she had witnessed some-one—a girl, it seemed—lurking in the distance; once in the barnyard when they'd first moved in and another time inside the house at the top of the stairs. On both occasions, she'd loudly made her disapproval known and ran full throttle toward the trespasser, and both times it seemed as if the girl disappeared into thin air. She nervously sniffed the ground where the trespasser had stood, but there was no scent. No footprints. No nothing.

But all was forgotten now as she and Violet watched Molly pull out a bag of doggie treats from the cupboard. Suddenly, a big clap of thunder caught all three of them off guard.

The crystal-blue, sunny, summer afternoon was being taken over by angry, black storm clouds churning overhead and a jagged streak of lightning in the not-too-distant horizon.

Within minutes, rain mixed with marble-sized hail pounded the roof. Another round of roaring thunder and a bolt of too-close lightning and the electricity went out.

"Well, girls," Molly said after an hour of no lights, "it looks like we're at the mercy of Mother Nature tonight."

Fumbling through the refrigerator for a snack, all she found was a moldy dish of macaroni and cheese left over from who knows when and a half-eaten Snickers candy bar. Her stomach growled. Breakfast had been eight hours ago, and she'd fooled around and skipped lunch. She was regretting that now.

She reached for the candy bar, threw the wrapper in the trash, and popped the whole thing in her mouth. She dug through the pantry, hoping for a bag of chips, pretzels, anything to hold her over till the power came back on and she could whip up some vittles. Nothing.

The dogs sat side by side on their back legs, watching Molly rummage through all the cabinets.

She picked up the phone and dialed the Powder Horn Restaurant, a country dive that was about a half a mile away at the end of Molly's dirt road and the corner of Highway 32. Three times she dialed, and three times she got a high, shrill busy signal.

"Their power must be out too," Molly said, looking right straight at Sally, who stood up and whined.

"Let's call Jenn and see if she's working."

"Annie's Restaurant," Jenn answered on the first ring.

"Oh good, y'all have power!"

"Only because Richard has a generator. Mr. Tightwad is scared to death he might miss out on a penny."

"I heard that!" Richard shouted in the background.

Ignoring him, Jenn continued, "Everybody else up and down Fifty-four is all closed up—even the Pitt Stop next door."

"Then I'm on my way." Molly grabbed her billfold and keys. "Right now a double cheeseburger with crinkly fries sounds like heaven."

"I'll go ahead and put your order—"

Pop! The line went dead. A booming clasp of thunder and another huge lightning bolt hit the cell phone tower.

"Cuh-rap!" shouted Molly, scaring poor Violet and causing Sally to sit up in full alert. Now the rain was coming down harder, so hard that you couldn't even see the steps at the end of the porch. There was no way anyone was going out in that weather.

Giving up on a decent meal, Molly once again fumbled around the pantry, this time for matches and candles, but was pleasantly surprised to find a flashlight with a new set of batteries instead. The house was starting to get hot, so she cracked the windows just enough to catch a breeze but not let the rain in.

After about thirty-five minutes, the nasty storm passed, revealing a beautiful starlit summer night; and if it hadn't been for the fat raindrops clinging to the trees, ground, and other objects, you'd never believed the ugly weather had even happened—except for the fact that there was still no electricity, which meant no air conditioning.

Molly shined the flashlight outside the kitchen window to the thermometer. Ninety-two degrees. Add about 70 percent humidity to that, and you can just about imagine how hot that house was. She took a quick shower to cool off and afterward pulled one of Scott's old cotton tees over her damp hair.

Molly patted the bed—her signal for Sally that it was bedtime—and then she bent over, picked up Violet, and placed her gently at the foot of the bed. She fell back onto the king-size mattress and began to say her prayers, but she was so exhausted that she was snoring before she even got to the "amen."

Quicker than you can say "sweet dreams," all three were sawing logs and lost into dreamland.

Fifteen minutes later, Molly sat up with a start at the sound of Sally barking wildly.

"What is it, girl?" she whispered, following Sally's line of vision out the open window.

Creeeaakkk, creeaakkk.

She grabbed the dull kitchen butter knife she'd used earlier to pry open the back of the flashlight to add the batteries. Cautiously, without making a sound she slid across the bed and gently lifted the edge of the lace curtain, scared to death of what she might see.

Then, she let out a sigh of relief, lay her head back down, and reached her arm across to gently caress Sally's back.

"Calm down, Sally. It's just the porch swing blowing back and forth in the wind."

As the rhythmic creaking continued, Molly lay back down, too exhausted to notice that there wasn't the slightest hint of a breeze.

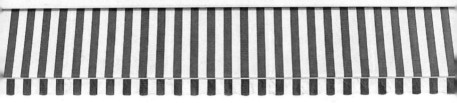

Chaos at the Committee

The next morning while Molly was scratching her head wondering why the blinds throughout the house were wide open when she knew darn good and well she'd closed every last one—the folks at the revitalization committee were downtown at the Wayside Inn Museum for their weekly planning session.

The meeting started out peaceful enough. Well, as long as you don't count the *not* unusual childish outburst between Michael and Winthrop—something about Michael telling Winthrop that "real" men don't wear loafers with buckles and no socks, and Winthrop telling Michael that the newspaper's comic section should forget comic strips and just print pictures of him.

Other than that, the meeting was getting off to a real fine start. The group had grown significantly, and as Wilhelmina predicted, most of that growth came from Brother Jeff's female admirers. To be fair, though, Mayor Thurman also made good on his promise to bring his councilmen on board.

Cool as a cucumber (but secretly so thrilled by today's crowd that she could burst), Wilhelmina stepped up to the podium and gently tapped the gavel.

"Let's call this meeting to order." Looking as elegant as ever in her navy skirt suit, posture perfect, a slight smile formed on her lips as her eyes scanned the room. She estimated at least twenty-five people and made a mental note to get an exact count before they adjourned.

As the room got quiet, Winthrop, not giving two hoots about parliamentary procedure, didn't waste any time making himself right at home.

"I've got a fabulous idea for a fundraiser!"

First of all, no one in our neck of the woods—especially someone who fancies himself to be a ladies man— uses the word *fabulous*. Nor, for that matter, do the men 'round here wear madras-print pants with a matching bow-tie—which served as pure fodder for Michael, who was still smarting from the Rusty Jug incident.

"I've got a fabulith idea," he mocked in an affected feminine voice and lisp. He was just itching to start a fight, which would have worked except for the fact that the normally meek and mousy Rosemary Hunter burst through the door screaming something that you *do* hear a lot of around here.

"Lord Jesus, help us all!" the poor woman was white as a sun-bleached cotton sheet. "You're never in a million years gonna believe what's happened."

Before anyone could ask what in tarnation was going on, she started sobbing. "We're all going to hell—straight to hell, I tell you." She paced back and forth. "Why, I can't go to hell! Do you hear me? I just can't! I have a baby girl waiting on me in heaven—I tell you I simply can't go to—"

Anne-Donovan Worthington stood up and rushed to Rosemary. I think she wanted to slap her—you know, like they do in the movies when they want to get someone to calm down. But instead, she just grabbed her by the shoulders and gave her a little shake. "Rosemary, settle yourself! Now what's going on? Why do you think we're all going to hell—besides the fact that most of these people here haven't seen the inside of a church building since Roosevelt?"

"It's Roy Bob Benson, y'all," Rosemary said in between sobs. "He just put a contract on the old Hacker's Jewelry building. He's turning it into a-a-a girly bar!"

At first you could've heard a pin drop. *Dead silence.* Then all of a sudden the place turned into an utter madhouse with everyone talking at once!

Wilhelmina slapped her gavel, trying to bring some type of order. It was no use.

"That Roy Bob Benson always was a no-good scoundrel!" one of the councilman said.

"Why, I never!" huffed one of Brother Jeff's older church women as she plopped her fat backside down in the chair and started fanning herself. Several of the other church ladies started to cry, and old Mrs. Smith tried, unsuccessfully, to lead the group in prayer.

"Whirly bar? What's a 'whirly bar'?" Ernie Harris had forgotten to turn his hearing aid on.

Soon all eyes and voices turned toward the mayor.

"He can't do that! There's gotta be a law against places like this!"

They all had poor Mayor Thurmond backed against the wall. All he could see were angry faces inches from his. Their unified voices were so loud and so strong and all jumbled up to where couldn't make sense of any of their words at all.

"Okay, let's all stay calm and…" Brother Jeff tried in vain to push some of the folks away to give the mayor some space.

Tap! Tap! Tap! Wilhelmina pounded the gavel. Rosemary continued pacing and sobbing about going to hell, the committee continued to rail on the mayor as he wiped his now-sweaty brow with a handkerchief, and poor Ernie Harris said for the umpteenth time, "Will someone please tell me what a whirly bar is!"

He thought maybe it was one of those new-fangled ice-cream places his granddaughter Lydia had told him about, but then why in the heck would everyone be so up in arms over something like that? Weren't they *trying* to bring new businesses to town?

Anne-Donavan, who'd had just about enough of all this, reached over to his ear, flipped the button on his hearing aid, and screamed, "*Girly* bar, Ernie—a *girly* bar! You know—a *strip club!*"

There. Someone said it. The dirty words. *Strip club.* Just as suddenly as the ruckus had begun, it ended.

Dead silence.

Everyone gathered their senses and went back one by one to their seats. The mayor relaxed, straightened his shirt, and trudged to his seat at the front of the room. Even Rosemary had calmed down a bit. Oh she was still crying all right, but at least she wasn't squalling like she was a few minutes ago.

Ernie rubbed his ear as he gave Anne-Donavan the evil eye. "You didn't have to shout, you know!

Strip club. These things happen in other places. Big places like Springfield or Kansas City—maybe even Joplin, but not in little old Eldo.

"Ladies and gentleman, we need to acquire all the facts before we rush to judgment," Wilhelmina stated matter-of-factly, hoping beyond all hope this was some big misunderstanding. She was perturbed at everyone's reaction to Rosemary's outburst to begin with. Didn't they realize how overly sensitive the dear woman was? The poor thing hadn't been the same since losing her daughter, Ashley, two years ago. Wilhelmina wanted the facts, all right, but she'd have to handle Rosemary with kid gloves.

"Now, Rosemary dear, please tell me why on earth you believe that Mr. Benson is opening up a-a"—she couldn't bring herself to say it—"this 'establishment.'"

Rosemary sat stoically on the front row, Kathryn on the opposite side of Wilhelmina with a protective arm around Rosemary's shoulder. All eyes focused on Rosemary, everyone on the edge of their seats so as to not miss a word.

"Because I heard it with my own ears!" Rosemary said as she started to cry again.

"Now, now, darlin'," Kathryn cajoled. "Just take your time."

Rosemary wiped away the tears with the back of her hand.

"I'm sure you all—or most of you all know that after Ashley… Well, we sold the farm and moved to town, and David took a job selling real estate with Max Montgomery."

Max Montgomery was the most successful real-estate broker in Cedar County, plus he owned a lot of those old boarded-up storefronts I told you about earlier—the Hacker building being one of them. Max also had a reputation as a shyster of sorts, so when he offered David a job, Rosemary had her reservations. She didn't tell David her doubts because it was the first thing she'd seen him halfway excited about since their beloved Ashley had gone to meet her maker.

"Well, I stopped in during my lunch hour thinking maybe he'd want to break for lunch, but Mary Lou said he was out with a client. So I sat down at his desk to leave him a note, and that's when I heard everything! I wasn't eavesdropping, I swear!" She looked at Kathryn then Wilhelmina and everyone else as if it were the most important thing in the world for them to know she would never listen in on a private conversation. "They were talking so loudly, I could hear every single word!"

It was also common knowledge that Roy Bob Benson didn't have a pot to pee in. So Wilhelmina wasn't alone in thinking that he had help in funding this endeavor, and it was probably in the form of Max Montgomery himself.

•

By five o'clock that evening, half the population of El Dorado Springs was stomping through the intersection of Main and Spring Streets waving picket signs and the like.

Roy Bob Benson sat behind the wheel of his black Ford flatbed chewing on a straw and smiling his tobacco-stained gleeful grin as he witnessed the sheer panic. He chuckled as he turned the key and revved the motor.

"Y'all can cuss and fuss all you want, but mamas, you better lock up your boys. 'Roy Bob's Babes' is fixin' to be open for business."

He threw the truck into gear and peeled rubber, confident that he had the world—or at least Cedar County—by the tail.

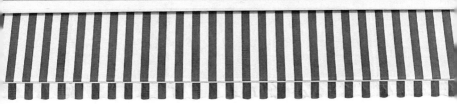

Not So Fast, Roy Bob

Roland Thurman, just moments away from reciting the oath of office as governor of the great state of Missouri, proudly placed his right hand on the old Bible that was a gift from his grandmother when he graduated from the University of Arkansas. The beautiful and award-winning actress Halle Berry stood close beside him, gazing at him adoringly, her red, sequin gown hugging every curve. The chief justice nudged him, reminding him of the important task at hand. Halle whispered softly in his ear that there would be time for "that" later as she moved just ever so slightly closer.

The adoring voices of his public rang out, sweetly, in the background. "Ro-land! Ro-land!"

"Roland! Roland!" He felt an annoying tap-tap-tap on his shoulder and then someone violently shaking him back and forth. "Wake up!"

"What? What?" He sat up in bed, removed his eye mask, and found himself nose to nose, looking straight into the wild eyes of his wife, Betty. She wore an orange moo-moo with pink rollers in her hair, her false teeth lying in a jar beside the bed looking as if they were smiling at him. Roland plopped back down, pulling the covers over his head, and clamping his eyes shut, desperate to get back to Halle Berry. Betty wasn't having it. She yanked the covers back.

"All these people are marching through our yard. They're going to stomp on my roses! Do something, Roland!"

Roland angrily threw the covers back and jumped to his feet, cursing under his breath. He grabbed his robe and thrust it on with the intensity of a soldier ready for battle. What in the heck did these people expect him to do? Didn't he make it perfectly clear that he'd gone over the city's bylaws with a fine-tooth comb? There was absolutely nothing that stated Roy Bob—or anyone else for that matter—could not open up a strip bar. The only stipulation was the business had to be legal. No drugs. No moonshine. No gambling. *And no hanky-panky!*

Roland got the surprise of his life when he stepped out on the portico. Gigantic news trucks from Joplin, Springfield, Kansas City, and some as far away as St. Louis and Tulsa were lined up as far as the eye could see on the street in front of his house. The old codger wasn't much of a morning person anyway, and the loud hum of the generators hooked to the news trucks, a dozen microphones being crammed in his face, and the sight of pesky reporters trampling his flower garden—even if one of them was that pretty Lisa Rose from Channel 3—didn't do anything to lighten his mood.

Just when he thought things couldn't be worse, he heard what sounded like a drum cadence in the distance, followed by the sounds of a disgruntled mob. Sure enough, within seconds he could see signs bobbing up and down and hear angry voices chanting and increasing in volume as they got closer. The Bulldog Marching Band was following close behind playing the "El Dorado Fight Song" in between intervals of "Shall We Gather at the River."

In less than three minutes what seemed like the whole town of El Dorado Springs had descended on his front yard, led by the revitalization committee. Kathryn McCarty was impossible to miss, with her watermelon-red suit, matching hat, and three-inch heels. Jerry Ray Turner was a sight to see himself, with his long, curly hair done up in a French twist, wearing an off-the-shoulder tank top, short denim skirt, and fire-engine red cowboy boots. Even Michael and Winthrop had put their feud aside long enough to come together for the sake of the town's reputation.

I have to admit in this case Michael made the biggest sacrifice by not voicing his opinion that Winthrop would probably have been one of Roy Bob's best customers. They were both on their best behavior, and much to the surprise of everyone, they worked side by side not uttering a word other than "pass me a nail" or "I need the hammer."

Peggy was at the rally, although she didn't march, and she didn't carry a sign. Once again she went unnoticed, and although the town didn't know it yet, she played a significant part in the day's activities.

No one had bothered to question how the news had broken so fast throughout the state and why all the press folks were there. Not even her husband, whose main goal in life was to source a lead story on the AP wire—or the Missouri Net News at the very least—had paused long enough in the midst of the panic to realize that this was the news story to break all news stories. But she had.

She would wait until just the right time to tell Michael that she was the one who'd had the clarity of mind to rally every major news source in the area. She closed her eyes for a moment and imagined him dropping his pen and pad to the floor, gathering her in his arms, declaring his undying love, and planting the most romantic kiss ever on her lips. Maybe for once he could see her value, and it would no longer matter that she wasn't the beauty that Constance was, and maybe, just maybe he would realize that she, Peggy, was the true blue love of his life.

"Excuse me," a familiar voice stunned Peggy back to reality. Startled, she flipped around and found herself staring into the eyes of none other than Channel 10's star anchor, Jessica Williams. With her shiny brunette hair and smooth, flawless skin, it was easy to see why she'd been named one of Springfield's Top Ten Most Beautiful Women by 417 Magazine. And while Miss Williams only wanted to ask Peggy a few questions, mainly to make sure she had the correct names of the key players and if she had any idea where she might be able to find Roy Bob Benson to get a comment from him, Peggy began to hatch a plan. Poor Jessica Williams. She'd just come to this little hole in the wall to report the news. She had no clue she was about to create a monster and change the course of someone's life.

•

Meanwhile, Molly was back at the ranch, listening carefully as she and her parents sat at the round, maplewood kitchen table that had once been her grandmother's. That old piece of wood had seen its fair share of hatched plans through the years, and Molly listened intently as Wilhelmina and Harrison poured out theirs.

When they finished, they look at her questioningly.

"Of course I'll do it!" she agreed at once. "We have no other choice!"

•

Roy Bob Benson pounded his fist on Max Montgomery's desk so hard that the glass wall shook. "What do you mean the deal is off? We had a contract!"

Mary Lou, Max's secretary, positioned her hand on the phone, ready to call the sheriff just in case things got ugly. It wasn't like Roy Bob had a stellar reputation. The last time he'd lost his temper, the object of his tantrum ended up with a broken nose, cracked jaw, and two broken ribs, and Roy Bob spent a month in the city jail.

Max was understandably nervous but desperately trying not to let it show. He remained calm, but sweat beads gathered on his forehead just below his hairline.

"The contract was contingent on you coming up with the money in the allotted time frame and on the premise that you weren't outbid," Max said, wiping his face with a napkin left over from lunch.

"I have three days to come up with the money before that contract runs out! Three days! And you're supposed to inform me when someone comes in with a higher bid!"

Max cleared his throat. "I would have, but there was no need to let you know."

"Whaddya mean there was 'no need to let me know'?"

Max hesitated, bracing himself for the outburst that was sure to come. "The new buyers doubled your offer."

Max held up his hand and raised his voice to cover Roy Bob's would-be objections, "They are willing to go above and beyond anything you have to offer, Benson, and they have the means to do it. You can't win at this game."

For probably the first time in his life, Roy Bob Benson was totally speechless. He was beyond furious as he took both hands and wiped Max's desk clean of the stacks of papers and real estate books. Pencils and papers went flying, and the heavy books hit the floor with several loud thuds.

Roy Bob shoved the door open, and as he stomped out he could be heard screaming that when he got his hands on the no-good, dirty rotten scoundrels that had robbed him, he'd make them pay. From the vibration of the building as he slammed the front door, no one doubted that for a minute.

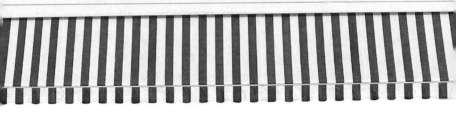

New Beginnings

The empty building smelled of mice, dust, and old papers. The heat was stifling. Scott McCarty entered first just to make sure there were no critters or creepy-crawlies lurking about then gave Molly and Jennifer the all clear.

"It's hotter than the day Sherman burnt Atlanta," he muttered as he wiped his eyebrow just in time to catch a drop of sweat before it dripped into his eye.

He'd come home early for the district work period to scout out the town's problem even though this was clearly out of his control. One thing he'd learned early in his political life was to not weigh in on an issue that wasn't his. Nope, best to let Billy Long, the new congressman from Springfield, and Mayor Thurmond take the heat on this one. But as soon as he'd gotten the text from Molly that she and her parents had decided to step in and buy the building out from underneath Roy Bob, he took the next flight home. Roy Bob had a well-deserved reputation for having a nasty temper. Scott wanted to be home just in case the old coot decided to start something with Molly.

"What in the world are you going to do with this place?" Jenn wrinkled her nose in disgust, tiptoeing slowly across the threshold. The hot air escaped from the building and smacked her in the face, for a moment taking her breath away. She stepped back and then very gently tiptoed in. Not only were there loose boards with nails sticking up, but she was scared to death of whatever was responsible for those little brown droppings scattered about.

"Molly, you didn't tell her?" Scott pulled the heavy glass door closed but immediately opened it back up and placed a wooden make-shift stop to keep it open in hopes of getting a breeze circulating.

"Tell me what?" Jennifer asked, stepping back toward the door. She was sweating like a pig. Her makeup was starting to melt. Molly wasn't fazed at all by the heat, and she wasn't the least bit intimidated by mice, possums, or any other creepy-crawly varmints that might be waiting in the rubble. This is what wellington boots were for.

"I'm thinking of a restaurant or a coffee shop," she answered, scraping her rubber boots to move a pile of dust for a closer look at the hardwood floors. Alice Hacker had put in new flooring when she'd first opened the jewelry store. Molly had heard that she'd taken wood from the Old Cruce Mansion—a house built by the founding father Nathanial Cruce—when it had been torn down in the seventies and placed in the store. She hoped the floor hadn't been ruined when the movers had come in and packed up the store merchandise for its move to the next town, Nevada (pronounced Neh-VAY-duh).

Jenn fanned her face with her hand. "When are you going to have time to run a restaurant? You've been so busy on that farm and with your dad's ranch that I've hardly seen you at all since you moved back. Why, your mama was complaining to me the other day that she can't even get you to join the revitalization committee."

Molly smiled as she walked over to Scott and took his hand in hers and told Jenn, "I'm not going to run it. You are."

Jenn stopped fanning herself and looked at Molly like she had lost her mind. "What are you talking about?"

"You heard me. I want you to run it." Molly put her hand up to block Jenn's objection. "When Dad, Mom, and I discussed this, our first thought was just do what we had to do to keep it out of Roy Bob's hands. Then we tried to figure out what to do with it once we bought it. Mother thought it would be a good antique store, and it probably would, but the more I thought about it, the more I envisioned a small café—a place where folks could come in and have breakfast, lunch, and maybe a piece of pie and shoot the breeze in the afternoon, and then be closed by five."

"Closed by five?" That right there sealed the deal for Jennifer. She'd worked at Annie's Restaurant for the past twelve years, working six days a week, from ten in the morning to ten at night—sometimes later. She squealed with delight, clapping her hands and kicking her long, brown legs, but then came straight back down to earth when she asked about the pay.

"I'll match what Richard's paying you," Molly promised.

"Plus," Scott piped in, "we'll have the contractor spruce up the upstairs apartment as soon as they get the downstairs finished. Part of your benefits will include living here rent-free."

"We'll give you a few days to think it over," Molly added.

"Done!" Jennifer blurted before they could change their mind. "There is absolutely nothing to think about! I am in like Flynn."

She hopped excitedly in place, clapping her hands and giggling like a high school girl whose crush had just asked her to the prom. Molly hopped and skipped over the loose boards and debris, her wellies clunking as they hit the ground, straight into Jennifer's arms. They were squealing and both talking at once, so they didn't hear the "Dixie" ringtone on Scott's Blackberry.

"Ladies! I hate to walk away from your little love-fest, but I've got a conference call in a few minutes. I'm going to have to head to the house." He tipped his head to Jennifer and blew Molly a kiss.

"I'll be home in a few minutes," Molly promised. "I want to let her see the apartment."

"The place isn't much yet," Scott said, which was very much an understatement.

"Are you kidding?" Jenn exclaimed. "I've been living in that tiny one-room apartment over by the school for going on six years now. Any place has to be better than that. Plus, after hours I'll have the whole building to myself. Heaven."

"Well, once the contractors rewire and fix the flooring, you go down to Producer's Grain and pick out whatever color paint you like." Scott winked. "Make this place home."

•

Home. Scott sighed. Pulling in to the long, winding driveway, canopied by maple tree branches matched up perfectly on both sides, he caught a glimpse of movement in his peripheral vision. Jerry Ray.

It took a lot of convincing on his wife's part for him to believe that his former football team captain was now wearing women's clothing. But sure enough, there in broad daylight was Jerry Ray in the flesh, all dolled up in a red jumpsuit, pant legs tucked in to cowboy boots, and his long hair pulled back in a ponytail.

Scott now remembered from one of Molly's e-mails that there was a problem with the lights on the horse trailer. Jerry Ray, toolbox at his side, turned to wave, and Scott noticed he was wearing an apron to protect his outfit from grease and dirt.

Scott waved back, fighting the urge to laugh out loud and wondering why Jerry Ray didn't wear a pair of coveralls like all the other mechanics in town, but then again had to remind himself that Jerry Ray was nothing like the other mechanics in town.

"Good to see you, my friend! I've got a conference call here in a sec, but are you gonna be around for a while?"

"At least another twenty or thirty minutes," Jerry Ray called back in the familiar deep voice Scott remembered from their football days. "If I'm not here when you're finished, stop by the station."

"You got it!" Scott grabbed his suitcase from the back seat. Both dogs eagerly trailed him, both wanting to be the first to be petted and scratched.

Sally patiently sat and waited, panting heavily, while Violet yapped and scratched the bottom of his pant leg. He bent over and scratched under her chin and then called for both dogs to follow him.

"Come on, girls. Let's go inside where it's cool." He turned toward the house, lugging his suitcase behind him, taking in the view of the place, wishing he could spend more time in this peaceful oasis.

Glancing to the top dormer, which was the window to his office, he saw clear as day, the face of a pretty young girl looking out the window. They made eye contact, and she smiled at him.

Hmmm, Molly must have changed her mind about hiring a cleaning lady.

He entered the air-conditioned house and halfway expected to see the girl, or at least hear her as she went about her duties. He didn't see hide nor hair of her on the main floor, and she wasn't in his office, either. He listened for a moment, but it was completely still.

Looking at his watch, he picked up the phone and dialed Washington, making a mental note to ask Molly about it later. But "later" found him wrapped in his wife's arms making up for lost time. By week's end, the girl in the window was the last thing on Scott's mind.

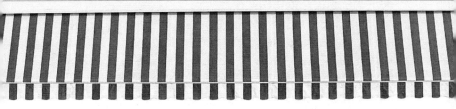

Trouble

"How about 'Molly-Moos'?" The grand opening was less than a week away, and the girls were racking their brains, trying to come up with a catchy name for the café.

"No way." Molly shot the suggestion clean out of the water. "People don't need to know who owns this place."

Jennifer gave a quick snort. "Please. This is El Dorado. Everybody knows everything around here. There are no secrets. Besides—look over yonder."

There was Ollie Griffin standing knee-deep in the park water fountain, scrubbing himself clean from head to toe. The soap slipped from his hands, and when he bent over to pick it up his backside was facing all of Main Street.

Molly shrugged. "At least he's wearing underwear this time."

"No, not Ollie." Jenn pointed straight south toward Spring Street. "Over there, across the street and to the right."

Roy Bob Benson was staggering up the sidewalk, looking more disheveled than usual, pausing every couple of steps to put the whiskey bottle he was carrying to his lips, tipping it straight up. Even Ollie stopped washing long enough to witness the animated antics of a highly intoxicated Roy Bob.

"Good grief—it's not even ten in the morning!" Molly said in disbelief.

"And if I was a bettin' woman, I'd make a bet he's headed straight here," Jennifer said, both of them motionless. "Should I call the police?"

"No, not yet," Molly answered, immediately questioning her own judgment as he got closer.

Roy Bob stumbled his way across Main Street, slamming his now-empty bottle of Jack Daniels to the sidewalk, where it broke into a million tiny slivers. He jerked the door open so hard that it bounced back, springing it with such force that later Jennifer would have to pay one of the contractors to replace the hinges.

"Now, Roy Bob, we don't want any trouble here."

Despite Molly's brave tough-girl act, it was obvious she was scared.

"Well, you shoulda thought o' that before you stole this place out from underneath me!" he slurred. He almost fell over backwards but leaned up against the wall to steady himself.

He regained his posture, pointed at Molly, but before he could take another step, Terry McCallister, manager of Carl's Gun Shop, popped in the door.

"Everything okay in here?" He'd sped across Main Street lickety-split when he saw the speed in which the whiskey bottle had met the sidewalk.

"Mr. Benson was just leaving." Molly was trying to give Roy Bob an easy out.

"I just g-g-got here, and I can d-do what I jolly well p-please!" The man was furious, and I'm sure if he hadn't been drunk, or at least if Terry hadn't been there, there's no telling what might have happened.

When old Roy Bob releases his fury, he is no respecter of persons—or gender, for that matter. Three of his four ex-wives have all ended up at Cedar County Memorial at one time or another with cuts, bruises, or broken bones. They were too scared to tell the sheriff what had happened, so Roy Bob was never punished.

Cindy Lou, his fourth wife, picked up a butcher knife in the midst of one of his drunken beatings and stabbed him in the chest, barely missing his heart and a major artery. Some have said maybe there wasn't a heart in there to stab, which I suppose would make sense as it only took him a little over a week to recover.

"Mr. Benson, I can either call you a cab or I can call the police." Molly reached in her pocket for her cell phone. "Which will it be?"

"Molly, don't worry about it," Terry insisted. "I'll take him outside with me, and I'll call the cab to take him home."

Roy Bob went willingly, but he was screaming to beat the band and pumping his fist wildly in the air, using some pretty colorful language.

"You'll be s-s-sorry you crossed me!" was the last thing he said as Terry stuffed the man's sorry carcass into the back of the taxi.

"Okay." Molly took a deep breath and turned her attention back to Jennifer as if nothing had happened. "Now. Where were we?"

"Um…naming the café."

"Yes, naming the café." Molly snapped her fingers. "I've got an idea! What if we had a contest, and who-ever comes up with the best name wins a free slice of pie every day for a whole year?"

Jennifer, still badly shaken up, managed a smile. "I think that's a brilliant idea!"

"Great! Then you have Michael put an announce-ment in the paper, and I'll stop by KESM on the way home and have Anne-Donavan put something on the radio."

•

Molly tossed and turned that night, which was very much unlike her. Usually she was zonked out the minute her head hit the pillow, but tonight she felt very uneasy. The truth of the matter was, she was afraid of Roy Bob. But it wasn't just him. There was no way he had the means to buy that building on his own. He didn't have a job that anyone knew of, and he really didn't even have a home of his own. It was common knowledge that Roy Bob was a squatter—he simply moved a bed into what was once known as the 8-Mile Tavern where Highways 32 and 97 forked. It had gone out of business in the midnineties.

Nope, Roy Bob was just a tool—a tool for someone who had the money to front the strip club but was too much of a coward to do it out in the open. But who?

She looked at the clock.

Good grief! It's almost midnight! I have got to get some sleep!

She forced her eyes shut in hopes of drifting off, but the sudden ringing of her bedside phone startled her.

Who's calling at this hour? Her first thought was Scott but then quickly dismissed it. Washington DC time was an hour ahead—he'd mostly likely have been asleep for hours. Maybe something had happened to Mother—or Daddy!

"Hello!" she said briskly into the phone, dreading the news she might hear on the other end.

Nothing.

"Hello?"

Still nothing, but she could hear breathing.

"Who is this?"

It was still quiet except for the breathing. She brought the receiver away from her ear to get a glimpse of caller ID: *Private Call.*

She put the receiver back to her ear, the caller's steady breaths letting Molly know they hadn't yet hung up. Molly was way too stubborn to be the one to give. Finally, after what seemed like forever, she heard the click as the phantom caller hung up.

She plopped her head on the pillow. Well, it didn't take a rocket scientist to figure out who that was. Either Roy Bob was just now waking up from the morning's drunken stupor, or it was the business partner that Molly would have bet her eyeteeth he was working with.

What's in a Name?

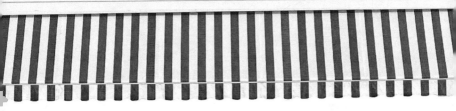

"Today's the last day to cast your ballot to name the new café opening up in a few days in what used to be Hacker's Jewelry," came the soft, soothing voice over the radio of almost every citizen in El Dorado Springs. "Grand prize will be a free slice of pie every single day for a year!"

Lisa Brown, KESM's star announcer, had been waking folks up in this town every morning for the past twenty-five years. Next to our girl, Sydney Friar, who is Miss Missouri, Lisa's the closest thing to a celebrity this town's got, which would explain why the next day Molly and Jennifer were literally going through hundreds of entries of people who wanted to win the grand prize.

"Hmm…" Jennifer mulled over the current entry in her hand. "The Dixie Dump."

"Are you kidding? It sounds like something you do after a big Sunday dinner," Molly answered, drumming her fingers on the bar.

Jennifer slipped the tiny piece of paper into the cup marked "Heck No," which was overflowing, and way more full than the one marked "Maybe," which was halfway full. The one marked "Serious Consideration"? *Completely empty.*

Jennifer dipped her hand into the Kansas City Royals baseball cap that held all entries neatly written and folded up on small pieces of paper.

"Good Eats."

"Boring."

"The Finer Diner."

"*Boring -er.*"

"Main Street Café"

"Not original…"

"One-Horse Town Eat 'Em Up Café"

"Too original. Plus, it sounds like we're serving horse meat. Gross."

"Pop's," Jennifer continued.

"Who the heck is *Pop*?"

"Cookie's."

"…or Cookie?" Molly was beyond frustrated.

"Ollie's Folley", Jennifer laughed. "Gee, I wonder who submitted that one!"

"Yeah, I wonder," Molly groaned, not seeing the humor. "Next, please."

"Chat 'n Chew."

"No."

"Hicks 'n Chicks."

"No!"

"Actually, I think that one is kinda cute," Jenn professed. Molly ignored her.

"How many do we have left?"

"Two," Jennifer answered, removing both slips of paper and placing the now empty cap on her head. She opened one, and her face turned beet red.

"Well, what is it?"

"I can't repeat it," Jennifer answered, which meant it must have been *really* bad because she did tend to cuss like a sailor at times.

"Let me see that." Molly yanked it from her hands. "How bad can it be?"

She read it, wadded it up, and threw it in the trash.

"I told you so," Jennifer said, unfolding the very last entry.

"Well, that's just great," Molly said huffily. "We're set to open in forty-eight hours, and we still don't have a name. If that don't beat all. You'd think out of all these mail-ins we'd at least have one that might possibly—"

"Oh brother, listen to this one. The Hillbilly Debutante Café. How stupid is that?"

"*What did you say?*"

"I said, 'How stupid is—'"

"No! Repeat the name!"

"The Hillbilly Debutante Café."

"That's it!" Molly snatched the paper out of her hand. She smiled; she'd know that handwriting anywhere. "That's our name. The Hillbilly Debutante Café."

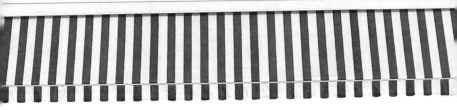

The Original Hillbilly Debutante

CONNECTICUT 1948

From the moment she made her grand entrance into this old world at seven pounds, five ounces, Wilhelmina's life had been defined by the expectations of others—her governess, the headmistress of her fancy boarding school, and of course her parents, especially her overbearing, egocentric father. But as the only child of Sheffield T. Wellington and his wife, Elizabeth, she was expected first and foremost to be a lady.

She was an exquisite beauty with ivory luminescent skin, and pale blue eyes framed by thick dark locks that cascaded down her back in ringlets. Born into extreme wealth and privilege, her formative years were under the strict regimen of her governess, Gladys Kepner, a cold, elderly lady who never once showed the child even the slightest bit of affection.

Wilhelmina only interacted with her mother occasionally, as Elizabeth Wellington was the toast of Connecticut society and had little use for things—or people—that kept her from being the center of attention. When Wilhelmina did get that rare opportunity to be near her mother, Elizabeth was no more generous in showing affection than the nanny. Wilhelmina adored her father, but unfortunately he too was emotionally detached from the young girl, and so she spent the first twenty-two years of her life desperately but unsuccessfully seeking his approval.

It was a lonely childhood, but as far as material things, she had the best of everything—riding lessons, etiquette classes, and a top-notch education starting with a private tutor during her grammar school years. At fourteen she was sent to boarding school at Miss Porter's School for Girls, where famous alumni Jacquelyn Bouvier Kennedy had graduated several years earlier.

Like Jackie before her (the similarity not unnoticed by Elizabeth), Wilhelmina made her official debut at the International Debutante Ball at the Waldorf Astoria in New York City. And also like Jackie, after graduating from Miss Porter's she was expected to attend Vassar College before marrying a suitable man from a family that would no doubt meet Sheffield Wellington's stamp of approval.

"I don't know why I'm expected to go to college," Wilhelmina wrote in her journal. "According to Mother, women of my 'station in life' don't have careers. We marry well, bear children, and spend our days lounging around, drinking tea, and gossiping with other women who have married well. Such a bore."

For Wilhelmina, a career was all she desired—a venue that would allow her to assert her independence and do something she *wanted* to do, not what she was *expected* to do. And that is exactly how she found herself at the University of Missouri.

Ever since she was able to put pen to paper and form sentences, Wilhelmina loved writing. Hidden in her closet behind rows of ball gowns and beautiful clothes, she had a basket full of diaries that she had kept, along with short stories and even a book that she had written in eighth grade.

While the other girls at school dreamt of their future husbands, Wilhelmina had dreamed of being a journalist. And all aspiring writers knew that the University of Missouri boasted the best journalism school in America.

It had taken much crying, pleading, and swearing she'd return to Berry Oak—the family's estate—the day after graduation before her father finally gave in. It was the only argument she'd dared had with him, and maybe that's why she'd won. It had taken him by complete surprise that she stood toe to toe and refused to take no for an answer, and Wilhelmina thought for one split second that she had seen just a tiny measure of pride in his eyes as he gave in.

Four years later, here she stood back in this house honoring that promise.

Harrison had insisted he accompany her even though she begged him not to. When they got off the train, he went his separate way to stay at the luxurious Delamar Hotel while she was driven home by Jules, her parents' trusted driver for the past twenty-five years.

"How bad can it be?" Harrison had asked her before they boarded the train in Missouri for the long trip to Connecticut. "When your parents see how much I love you and they know who my family is, they can't help but give us their blessing."

But Harrison didn't know her father. Sheffield Wellington didn't give a rat's behind that the Bermans were the wealthiest landowners in the state of Missouri or that Harrison already had a job lined up with his father's cattle company and would be able to care for her just as good, if not better, than the Van der Wold boy they'd had their sights on.

Her father had mentioned no less than a dozen times while she was growing up that James Van der Wold would no doubt inherit a position of high standing in his father's bank—an establishment that had been passed down since the 1700s, much like the manufacturing company owned by the Wellingtons, and how convenient it would be to merge the two families.

Announcing her intentions to marry Harrison Berman was worse than Wilhelmina expected. Her father's harsh, penetrating voice boomed throughout the halls, causing a near-collision of four nervous maids and a frantic butler, each desperate to find a place to hide. Harrison had been known to fire whoever was in sight during his infamous hissy fits and he was already on his second round of employees in the past 90 days.

Elizabeth feigned lightheadedness as if she were about to swoon. What would the ladies at the country club think if her daughter married a- a- *cowboy?*

"Look at what you are doing to your mother!" Sheffield's screams echoed, but Wilhelmina didn't flinch.

"If you would just give him a chance…" Wilhelmina remained calm. Elizabeth started to cry and removed a lavender flower-embossed handkerchief from her bosom and dabbed her eyes. "Mother, please don't cry. Really, I'm sure you'd love him if you just got to—"

"We don't want to get to know him!" Sheffield continued his tirade. "What on earth does he—that, that *simpleton, a farmer for God's sake*—have to offer my daughter?"

"He has a lot to offer, Father. Why, their family is much like ours…" which was the wrong thing to say because even though it *was* true, the last thing Sheffield wanted to hear was that an Ozark, hayseed, farm family could possibly hold a candle to a Wellington—a family that had been one of the first to arrive in this country!

By now, Elizabeth was wailing as if she'd sat on one of her expensive, exclusive hat pins. Between her father's rampage and her mother's near-hysteria, Wilhelmina couldn't hear herself think!

"Mother! Father! Please listen!" she pleaded. "Harrison's family is just as wealthy as we are! Their home," she said as she threw up her arms and looked around the estate home she'd grown up in, "is just like ours! Please, *please* give him a chance. He's here in town, and I am begging you to just try to get to know him a bit, and I know you'll love him just as much as I do!"

She really hadn't wanted to resort to that. What did it matter how much money the Berman family had or didn't have for that matter? She loved Harrison— she'd loved him almost the moment she'd laid eyes on him. He was so very different than the prep-school boys she'd known in Connecticut. He was strong from physical hard work. He always wore cowboy boots and jeans and had the most beautiful smile she'd ever seen. And no one had ever made her laugh or feel as loved as he had. And if that wasn't enough to make her fall hard—his parents' warmth and acceptance made her feel more at home and welcome than anyone ever had in her entire life.

Wilhelmina stood still, stoically defiant. "I am marrying Harrison Berman. Now, I would love to have your blessing, but if—"

Sheffield was every bit as stubborn.

"If you marry that redneck farm boy," he interrupted her. "I'll—I'll—"

"You'll what, Father?" Her lip was trembling. *Please don't make me choose.*

"I'll cut you off without a penny!" Wilhelmina winced at his brusque words.

"Then I suppose there is nothing left to say." She slowly turned toward the door, knowing she was walking away forever from her family, her home. Folks around here would have declared it a miracle when Elizabeth suddenly recovered from her near-fainting spell and stood straight up, strong as an ox.

"Sheffield! You don't mean that!"

Pausing with her hand on the door, ready to turn the handle and step out of their lives forever, Wilhelmina held out for one split second, praying that maybe, just maybe Sheffield would change his mind. But somehow she knew that even though he was caught up in the moment and might change his thinking later, this would be the last she ever saw of either one of them. Her father was too proud to admit he was wrong, and regardless of Elizabeth's outburst, Wilhelmina knew for certain her mother would never defy him.

"I meant every word!" Sheffield said. "I did not raise my daughter to be some—some—*hillbilly debutante!*"

Peggy Dailey's Debut

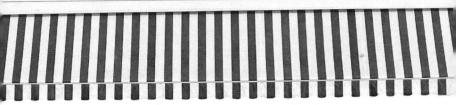

I t was crystal clear from the beginning that The Hillbilly Debutante Café was the new "it" place in El Dorado—where a person could get caught up on the latest gossip, visit with friends, and have the closest thing to a home-cooked meal without having to slave over a hot stove themselves.

Ollie was the first customer on opening day. He came over straight from his morning dip in the park fountain, wet hair slicked back and sporting nothing but a bath towel wrapped around his waist.

Jennifer laid down the law. "Ollie, this is not your own personal kitchen, and I don't need to see everything the good Lord gave you! Go back to your car and get some clothes on."

About five minutes later, he returned wearing his cleanest dirty shirt with a mis-matched pair of plaid shorts.

"I don't know which is worse," Jennifer muttered under her breath. "Purple and white stripes with green and navy plaid, or his half-naked bony body."

After about the first week, you could set your watch by different people that settled around the tables throughout the day.

Seven a.m. was the breakfast crowd—usually the same people on their way to work, stopping off for a quick cup of coffee and a sausage-bacon-cheese-biscuit and a side order of grits to go. The same group of farmers gathered around tables, taking a break from early-morning chores and settling down to a hot, stick-to-your-ribs-style breakfast.

Late morning, when the breakfast crowd was gone, Harrison Berman could be found sitting in the back booth taking advantage of the free slice of pie he'd won fair and square in the café naming contest. Folks scratched their heads when the announcement of the new name was broadcast over the radio. Then when they read the newspaper article Michael had written explaining exactly who the Hillbilly Debutante was and how the name had come to be, everyone marveled at the romantic bone Harrison had done such a good job of hiding through the years.

About ten minutes before noon, the lunch-bunch started trickling in. Sometime during the noon hour, diners would get their own private fashion show between Jerry Ray's glitzy get-ups and Kathryn's glamorous suits and hats.

Winthrop and Michael were part of the lunch crowd too; Winthrop because he had the hots for Jennifer, and Michael mostly because he hoped to overhear a morsel of gossip that might turn into a news lead. Both men, however, were read the riot act opening day.

"I will not hesitate to have you both thrown outta here on your hind ends if you so much as raise your voice!" Jennifer threatened. "Do you understand?"

They agreed, which was a good thing because I have no doubt Jennifer would have made good on her promise.

Wilhelmina didn't come in too often—only about once a week—but she did make it a point to drive by to see the "The Hillbilly Debutante Café" sign. Never did she look at that sign but what she didn't silently thank God for giving her the strength to walk away from the ghost of the lonely, unloved child she had once been, straight into a new life in a new part of the country where she had more love than she could shake a stick at.

The revitalization committee, of course, were the best customers, eager to support the new business and just pleased as punch that Roy Bob Benson had been successfully run out of town—figuratively, if not literally, as he was on many occasions seen driving past the café, honking his horn and flipping the bird as he wheeled by. It was the talk of the town for a while, but then as things have a way of doing, it got old and people stopped paying him any attention, figuring he'd get tired and give up.

Molly wasn't so sure about that, because she was still getting crank calls all hours of the night, and sometimes she witnessed him driving slowly past her house.

Jennifer had seen him at least three times, in his truck leering at her when she was locking up in the evening.

One day he carried things just a bit too far. He came to a screeching halt in the middle of Main Street and started howling and cussing so loud that Police Chief Jarod Schierreck, who just happened to be having lunch, went outside with the intention of telling him to move along before he was arrested for disturbing the peace but ended up arresting him for driving while intoxicated.

I guess that's the beauty of living in a small town. People think nothing ever happens around here, but you're always hearing of something amusing going on. And sometimes if you're lucky, you don't get to just "hear" about it but actually get to see it with your very own eyes.

Take, for instance, Wednesday a few weeks ago—The Hillbilly Debutante Café had only been open for about three or four days. It was lunchtime, and Jennifer; her mother, Ida, who's the cook; and Rosemary Hunter, whom she'd hired as the noontime waitress, were busier than a one-legged man at a butt-kicking contest. It seemed like just another ordinary day when in walked the most beautiful lady this town had ever seen.

No one would have noticed Michael Dailey following this woman around like a sick puppy until they heard his familiar voice, now a pathetic plea. "Peggy, please don't leave."

Peggy? Why on earth was he calling this woman Peggy? She was as far away from the too-skinny, too-pale, too-quiet, ever-so-plain, mousy Peggy as you could possibly imagine.

You could have heard a pin drop in that restaurant. All eyes were on that whine-bag Michael with everyone wondering why in the world he was calling her Peggy and begging her not to go until…

"Oh my gosh!" gasped Anne-Donavan, who was sitting at a table with her jealous, but equally awe-struck sister-in-law and leering, lecherous brother. She adjusted her thick-lensed, horn-rimmed glasses. "Peggy *Dailey*?"

How on earth she put two and two together and came out with Peggy Dailey was beyond anyone's guess, but sure enough—*it was Peggy!*

The mousy, brown, stringy hair had been colored a rich, buttery blonde and trimmed to just below her jaw line, giving a soft, feminine look to frame her face, which was now perfectly made up. Gone was the ruddy, splotchy complexion, smoothly covered up in a velvety, expensive Chanel foundation. For the first time, her aqua-blue eyes were piercing, thanks to the makeup lessons she'd learned when she slipped away to Kansas City and enrolled in the Patricia Stevens Finishing School. She'd told Michael she was taking an advanced photography class at Crowder College in Joplin, but instead had been under the strict guidance of the legendary Melissa Stevens, daughter of the late, great headmistress of one of the finest finishing schools in the country.

Melissa was an excellent teacher, and Peggy had been a most eager student. Dressed to kill, her skinny, scrawny body didn't look so skinny and scrawny, and if I was going to guess, judging by the clingy hot-pink jersey knit wrap dress she was sporting, I'd also say she'd had a couple of "things" enhanced.

Everyone's jaw dropped, and the look on Constance Worthington's face was absolutely priceless—which was not lost on Peggy. Dreaming of this moment was what had kept her going when she felt she was too exhausted to make the hundred-mile trek to Kansas City.

"Yes! It's me, all right." Her once meek voice was now forceful, almost angry. "Peggy Dailey! The woman who could fall off the face of the earth and no would ever notice! The woman who could disappear into oblivion and no one would blink an eye."

She did a 180-degree pivot, and, thanks to her new three-inch alligator pumps, she stood eye to eye to her husband. The husband who had humiliated her for years by always letting her know she wasn't his first choice; that he'd settled; the husband who had spent the past fifteen years pining away for another woman!

"I'm the woman who gave up on you ever loving me but at least tried to earn your respect as a colleague!" She quickly diverted her attention away from Michael and turned her anger on Anne-Donavan and the others—which was pretty much everyone—who had carried protest signs up and down Main Street and to the front step of the mayor's house.

"Who do you think alerted the media about the prospective strip club and all the mayhem erupting in this town? Who do you think organized the press releases, the interviews, the coverage on CNN, Fox, and all the major networks? It was *me*, people! *Me!*"

Just as quickly, it was back to a very embarrassed Michael. "All I wanted from you was a thank you. That's all. Well, guess what." Peggy changed to a cool demeanor, so calm it was almost scary. "I don't *need* your thanks—or your appreciation! The movers are coming Saturday to get my things. Jocelyn can stay here so she doesn't have to change schools. My attorney will be in touch to work out a joint-custody agreement.

"In case you miss me," she concluded with a snarky, sarcastic tone, "you can turn on Channel 3 KYTV in Springfield. I'm the new morning anchor."

Before trekking out the door, she stopped for a split second at Anne-Donavan and Constance's table. All the years of humiliation of living in Constance's shadow and being the victim of her catty comments and haughty looks had taken its toll on poor Peggy.

"How do you like me now?" Peggy asked her, basking in the red glow of Constance's face as it turned three shades of crimson.

It was quiet for a full thirty seconds after Peggy left. Although everyone was shell-shocked, I don't think anyone felt sorry for Michael. He'd been a jerk to Peggy from day one.

Finally the silence was broken by the echo of loud clapping coming from the back corner of the restaurant. Ollie, who had apparently snuck in the side door during the noon rush, was sporting nothing but a small bath towel barely covering his assets and giving Peggy the enthusiastic standing ovation she very much deserved.

More Trouble

"I can't smile without you… No, I can't smile without you… I can't laugh and I can't sing…"

Ah, classic Barry Manilow from the 1970s. And it also happens to be the obnoxious ringtone on Molly's cell phone.

"Hello?" It was 6:45. *No one calls this early. It's gonna be another heavy-breather phone call.*

But it wasn't. It was Jennifer—a panicked, hysterical Jennifer telling her to get herself down to the café, and right now.

It was 7:15 when Molly (with Sally in tow) arrived. A small group—the breakfast crowd—gathered outside The Hillbilly Debutante Café, and Molly's heart rate increased three-fold when she saw not only Police Chief Schierreck's car but Sheriff Ronald Starbuck's patrol car too. The two men were deep in conversation while one city policeman was taping off the area and the deputy was taking notes.

"Uh-oh, Sally, this doesn't look good." From Jenn's tone Molly had no idea what to expect, so her first instinct was to bring the dog along for protection just in case.

Sheriff Starbuck nodded and pointed at Molly's feet. "I see you wasted no time getting here."

In her haste, Molly had unknowingly put on two different kinds of boots—a Burberry on her left foot and a Hunter on her right.

She'd never cared about girly things or how she looked, and this certainly wasn't the time to start. "What's going on here? Were we robbed? Is anyone hurt?"

Before he could tell her no on all three accounts, she saw for herself what all the fuss was about—*in great big red letters.*

"Hillbilly Hore Howse" was spray painted all across the front glass. Molly was ready to spit nails, but she also couldn't help but laugh at the poor spelling.

"Another indication why a person shouldn't drop out of school in the sixth grade. The only reason he—*being Roy Bob, I'm sure*—was able to spell 'hillbilly' correctly is because he copied it off the sign!"

"I don't know when this happened; I didn't hear a thing!" Jennifer was crying. "Oh, Molly, I'm so sorry!"

Molly hugged her. "I'm so glad you're okay! I thought we'd been robbed or something!"

Michael Dailey was snapping pictures and jotting down notes. No doubt this would be the lead story on the front page of the *Sun* next week. A few minutes later, Lisa Brown from KESM pulled up with her microphone and recorder in hand ready to interview any witnesses. Unfortunately, it looked like Winthrop was beating Michael to the punch on the story since the printed word was always at least a day behind the spoken one.

"Molly, I'll have one of my guys come down later and measure, and we could have a new glass put in by the middle of next week," offered Drex Salazar of Dash Glass Repair.

She smiled. "Thanks, Drex. Just let me know how much, and I'll cut you a check the same day."

"Nope." He shook his head. "This one's on me. If it weren't for you, this place right here really would be a hillbilly whore house—no offense. On the hillbilly part, I mean."

"None taken." She hated to cry and very seldom did it, but she didn't even try to hold back. *This* was what she'd missed all those years living in Washington, DC. "But you really don't have to do that. I—"

"Nope, please…let me do this. Your family, especially your mother, is breaking her back to get this ghost town up and running. She's been this town's best cheerleader since she moved here. Let me honor her in this way. From what I hear, this place was named after her."

"Yes, it's a pet name my father has had for her for years." She sniffed and dabbed the tears from her eyes. "Thanks again, Drex. I appreciate this."

Big Scott, Molly's father-in-law—a large, John Wayne type of man, including the cowboy hat— reminded her that Missouri was a "right to carry" state and maybe she should start exercising that right.

"I don't think so, Dad. I've always been afraid of guns, and I'm afraid I'd end up shooting myself instead of the bad guy." And then another terrible thought crossed her mind. "Or I'd end up shooting Scott if he came home unexpectedly."

Molly knelt down and wrapped her arms around Sally's thick neck.

"Besides," she said, standing up and giving Sally one final scratch under the chin. "I've got my girl here to take care of me. Sally's never let me down; have you, girl? She once got a homeless man on the ground in DC—he got a bit too close. She didn't hurt him, but he never tried to harass me for change after that."

"I hate to interrupt," David Hunter said. "But has anyone questioned Ol' Ollie? Livin' in that car up there with nothin' to do, he knows everything that goes on 'round here. Maybe he saw somethin'."

"I'll send one of my boys up to have a talk with him later," Chief Schierreck said, although he doubted that Ollie Greene would talk even if he had seen anything.

Schierreck told the crowd, "If y'all hear anything around town—anything at all—let me or one of my men know. We'll investigate all leads."

"When can we open back up?" Molly asked.

"Anytime," the chief said. "The inside wasn't compromised, so please, by all means—"

"Y'all came here to eat, so come on in!" Molly motioned for everyone to follow her inside.

"I'll stay and help you all out," she assured Jennifer, Ida, and Rosemary, who, needless to say, were pretty shook up.

By noon the whole town was buzzing about the graffiti, which did absolutely nothing to hinder business.

They served an insane amount of food—the most profitable day they'd had since opening, which prompted Jennifer to joke at closing time that maybe they could put Roy Bob on the payroll to spray paint a different message on the storefront about once a month or so.

"Not funny," Molly said.

"Where's your sense of humor?" Jennifer asked.

"It left the building after about the fourteenth joke on my mismatched boots."

Ida and Jenn laughed. Rosemary didn't do much laughing these days, and the day's events had made her a nervous wreck, but she did manage to edge out a smile. All three ladies wondered why Molly didn't care a little bit more about her appearance—after all, she was a big shot senator's wife—almost like a first lady as far as they were concerned.

And right now this reluctant first lady was totally exhausted. Molly never doubted for a second that the girls worked hard, but today she had a whole new respect for them.

She pulled off Highway 54 onto the gravel road right next to the Powder Horn Restaurant, about three miles south of town. (Unlike The Hillbilly Debutante Café, the Powder Horn stayed open late for dinner.) She was tempted to pull in and order a prime rib dinner to go, but Sally, bless her heart, had been cooped up in Jennifer's upstairs apartment all day, not to mention poor Violet who'd been home alone for over seven hours without a potty break.

Dixie left a trail of dust as Molly drove her down the old dirt road toward home. Steering into the drive,

Molly noticed a delicate-looking young girl with long blonde curls, standing in the ditch, reaching over the fence to pet Joe, her seven-year-old quarter horse. The gelding was nuzzling his soft velvety nose against the girl's cheek.

Must be one of the neighbor's daughters, Molly thought, waving to the girl. She didn't recall seeing her before and thought it kind of strange but sweet that she was wearing a long pure white lace dress—it gave her an angelic quality, unlike the clothes, or lack-of, teenage girls were wearing nowadays.

The girl smiled, but she didn't wave back. When Sally sat up on her haunches and started barking furiously, Molly shushed her and glanced in the rearview window, hoping the girl wasn't startled by the dog's disapproval, but she was nowhere in sight.

"You should be ashamed of yourself scaring that poor girl."

Sally made a beeline for the road as soon as Molly opened the door, sniffed around the ditch, and came back up to the porch to stand guard.

When Molly unlocked the door, the smell of meat and vegetables roasting in the slow cooker permeated throughout the house. Before further investigation and finding that her bed had been made, her pajamas folded, and the mates to the mismatched boots she was wearing pushed neatly side by side, she tried to coax Violet outside so she could relieve herself after a long day of being inside. But the little dog didn't budge.

Apparently the person who had made the bed, cooked the meal, and even set the table to where all she had to do was sit and enjoy had also been thought-ful enough to let Violet out for her afternoon *constitu-tional*, as my daddy used to call it.

Oh yeah, Molly thought before she bowed her head to say grace. *There are definite advantages to having your mother live close by.*

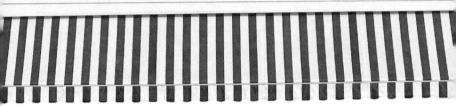

Whodunit?

"Well, darling, I'd love to take credit, but I've been in Jefferson City all day for a DAR conference." Wilhelmina may have been kicked to the curb by her snobby scoundrel father and her egocentric, pretentious mother, but she was still proud of her heritage and the fact that both of her eighth-great-grandfathers were patriots in the American Revolution. "I'm surprised you've forgotten. After all, I did stay after you for two weeks ahead of time to go with me. Really, darling, you won't join the revitalization committee but you should at least join the Daughters of the American Revolution. It is your birthright, after all."

Oh, not again.

"Maybe later, Mother." *There—give her hope. That will keep her off my back for a while.*

"Right now, I just want to know who came into my house. It had to have been someone who has a key because the door was locked—and absolutely no sign of forced entry!"

"Well, who all have you given a key to?" Wilhelmina wondered why Molly was making such a fuss. Only a handful of keys had been given out, so all she had to do was narrow down the few and—*voila!*—there was her answer.

Molly counted, "Let's see…I gave one to you and Daddy, one to Kathryn and Big Scott, Jennifer has one…and Scott, of course, has one. You were gone, Big Scott and Jennifer were with me, Scott's in DC, so that would leave either Daddy or Kathryn."

"Darling, your father couldn't make a bed if his life depended on it, and he wouldn't know a 'crock pot' if it were staring him in the face holding a loaded gun. It had to have been Kathryn, although she was supposed to be in Springfield today… I don't remember why. Well, that's neither here nor there—obviously she didn't go! I mean after all, who else could it be?"

Who else could it be was exactly what she was afraid of, although it would be highly unlikely that if Roy Bob wanted to get his revenge he'd clean her room and feed her a home-cooked meal. "Killing with kindness" didn't seem to be his style at all.

"Listen, Molly, I'm getting ready to drive through the Lake of the Ozarks, and I always lose phone—"

The line went dead.

On to Kathryn.

"No, sugar pie, it wasn't me. I've been at the quarterly trunk show at the Harem Boutique, you know that wonderful store on Glenstone in Springfield."

As if she doesn't have enough clothes already, Molly thought as she patiently listened to her mother-in-law drone on and on about all the wonderful things she'd purchased.

The Harem is one of those fancy boutiques that caters to all those socialite ladies in Springfield. Well, when Kathryn can't make it to Dallas, she spends a lot of her time at the Harem. They know her by name, and I'll bet her silver Range Rover could find its way there without her.

"Maybe it was your mama; that sounds like something she'd do."

"No, I've already checked with her. Thanks anyway, Kathryn."

"No problem, darlin'. Wish I could've been more help," Kathryn said. "Listen, when that son of mine comes home next time, we'll all have to get together. We'll invite your parents out to the house and have us a big barbeque. Texas-style!"

"Sure thing," Molly agreed, although a big family get-together right now was the furthest thing from her mind.

•

Chief Schierreck's interview with the diners that day didn't offer up any clues.

Considering the paint was dry by the time Jennifer came downstairs to open up at 6:40, the artist must have completed his masterpiece a good two hours beforehand.

The sidewalks pretty much fold up in this town at 5:00 p.m., so whoever did this was sure he'd have plenty of privacy at four in the morning.

Chief was hopeful that maybe Ollie had seen something suspicious or, if nothing else, as hot as it had been, his car windows would be open and he could have heard something.

"I can't hear anything with this loud thing goin'." Ollie pointed to a battery-operated fan perched atop the dashboard. He couldn't have possibly felt anything from those noisy, whirring blades because his old calico, Mo-Ped, had parked his lazy carcass on top of old yellow, musty newspapers stacked so high they reached the bottom of the headrest on the passenger's seat.

"Well, if you hear anything here on the street…"

Here on the street'? Where does this guy think he is—Chicago? Ollie tried to laugh, but it came out sounding like a thick, phlegm-induced cough.

"…just let me know." The chief turned to go back to his patrol car.

Ollie wanted to ask him how the heck he was supposed to get in touch with him since his place didn't exactly have a phone, but that awful coughing spell overtook him again.

"Hey, you okay?" Chief Schierreck asked. Ollie coughed and hacked until he almost couldn't breathe, and he clutched his chest. His face turned fire-engine red, and his body quivered. The chief reached for his radio to call an ambulance, but Ollie shook his finger in protest.

"I'm fine, I'm fine…" he insisted when his coughing subsided. "Put that silly thing away. I've just got a bit of a cold, that's all. I'll be fine."

The chief was hesitant about leaving him alone. That cough didn't sound like the cough from a cold, and besides, it was ninety-seven degrees. It was possible but highly unlikely that Ollie was suffering from a cold in July.

"Well, if you need anything, just call. Here's my card." He couldn't fathom the idea of someone not having at least a cell phone, not even Ollie.

Ollie didn't try to argue this time. He was afraid if he opened his mouth to speak the cough would come back and he wouldn't be able to stop and that pesky cop would force him to go to the hospital.

As for Schierreck, he made a mental note to come back and check on Ollie periodically over the next few days.

The Picnic

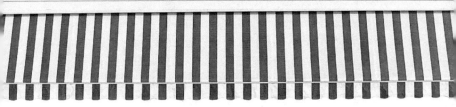

By the weekend, all talk of the graffiti had died down, and a new wave of excitement filled the air. It was time for the town's annual birthday celebration. The El Dorado Springs Picnic, hereby referred to as simply "the Picnic."

The Picnic takes place—come rain or shine—the third Thursday, Friday, and Saturday of every July. Forget every mental image you may have of picnics, because this is no *ordinary* picnic. No siree.

It's more like a homecoming. Anyone who has ever lived here plans their whole vacation around the Picnic. They come together for class reunions, family reunions, or just to walk up and down Main Street to show off, whether it be a significant weight loss, a new outfit, or a third wife.

Women start their diets in March and plan their picnic wardrobe in May (everyone except for Jerry Ray and Kathryn, who planned theirs on New Year's Day). The hair and tanning salons are booked up a whole month in advance. The Picnic, if you haven't figured it out yet, is a *big deal.*

Main Street—which is essentially Missouri State Highway 82—is completely shut down. If you happen to be an over-the-road trucker hauling who knows what to who knows where, then you'll have to follow the big orange detour signs through the tiny backstreets of town to Highway 54 to be on your merry way.

In front of the park across the sidewalk from the rock wall, the Lions, Kiwanis, and Optimist clubs sell corn dogs, hot dogs, sodas, and funnel cakes.

Farther down the street, little ones are perched atop horses on the merry-go-round while lovebirds sit side by side on the Ferris wheel. The more adventurous gather up the street a ways to ride the scrambler, the twirl, and other crazy rides where they can be flipped upside down, twirled on their side, and experience any other unnatural movements that may cause them to lose all remnants of the corn dogs, hot dogs, or funnel cakes they consumed earlier.

However, it's not all about throwing your hard-earned money away on rides or tossing darts at balloons to try to win your date a stuffed teddy bear.

The rock wall literally becomes invisible as people clamor to grab a seat. It's the best place in town to people watch. You have to get there pretty darn early to find a spot, but if you miss out—no worries—there is always the park.

My beloved grandmother—God rest her soul—and hundreds of others just like her, would get to the park around eight o'clock Thursday morning and park their lawn chairs in their favorite spot and leave them there till Saturday night—only occupying them at night just in time to listen to the city band and listen to whatever country music band is performing. The amazing thing about that? In all the history of the picnic—which started the year the town was founded in 1881—there has not been one single incident of someone coming in and stealing a spot already claimed. It just isn't done.

The few businesses located downtown completely close up shop those three days of the Picnic. If you're a restaurant, no way can you compete with corn dogs and the like, and nobody is going to shop for glass or floor covering that week. Everyone is just too focused on the Picnic.

Carl's Gun Shop stays open because it's a combination store and museum, and of course Bobby Joe keeps the Spring Street Tavern open. He makes more in that weekend than he does all year—go figure!

Since there are so many people all in one place at the same time, the Picnic tends to bring out every politician and every politician wannabe.

Last year, Molly had been in the foray as a candidate's wife since Scott had tossed his hat in the senate race. It was ugly. His opponent's campaign was based on family values, so he marched his wife and six kids to every debate throughout the district. Richard Roberts insisted that his success at managing a company that kept hundreds of people employed, coupled with his finesse of handling such a large family, made him the best candidate.

"My opponent is a just a kid—wet behind the ears!" Roberts' tirade was always the same. He'd chant like a Sunday morning southern evangelical preacher while his wife stood dutifully behind him. Their six little stair-step children were always dressed in identical outfits, like the kids in *The Sound of Music*. She was the epitome of the supportive wife, clutching her pearls and shaking her head in disgust. How dare Scott oppose her older, more powerful husband!

"He's just barely thirty years old, has no business experience, and seems to think just because he was on Senator Bond's payroll that entitles him to take over for him when he retires!" Roberts' obnoxiously loud, sing-song-y voice permeated the thick summer air, and about every third sentence a few of his faithful supporters would shout, "Amen!" The only thing missing was the hallelujah choir.

Keep in mind that although Scott is actually closer to forty, had managed every penny of Kit Bond's campaign funds, and for four years after that had been the senator's chief of staff, it still seemed that Roberts's misrepresentation of facts would win him the election.

Until, that is, he was slapped with a paternity suit by his secretary. When that story broke, another young woman came forward. Apparently he also had a child with her. No wonder he was preaching family values— he had three of them!

At the end of the day, although it was still by a pretty narrow margin, folks decided they'd rather have a wet-behind-the-ears-kid as their senator than an older, more experienced, cheating rogue.

Now that it was behind them, Molly looked forward to just being Molly at this year's celebration.

"Maybe you should wear a skirt," Scott suggested at the sight of Molly's knee-length khaki shorts and sneakers.

"What's wrong with this?" she asked. "It's a perfect outfit for the Picnic. And at least I'm not wearing my wellies that you hate so much. Besides, it's not like you're campaigning this year."

"Come on, Moll. You know how this works. We're always campaigning."

Molly wasn't giving an inch. "But this is home, Scott. *Home.* I don't have to impress anyone here."

He didn't say anything else. He didn't have to.

•

Molly looked cute as a button in her pink Lily Pulitzer shift dress, single strand of pearls, and gold Jack Rogers sandals left over from her days in DC when her lifestyle called for a more casual elegance. She even put on a coat of mascara and a dab of lip gloss—something she hadn't done since she left DC.

Dirty dishes leftover from supper cluttered the sink, and the laundry pile in the middle of the hallway seemed to taunt her as she slammed the front door and locked it. She hoped the mystery housekeeper would take a night off because she really didn't want to explain to Scott how things had miraculously tidied themselves up. Number one, she was in no mood to try to explain it to him and then him get all worried and worked up, but the real reason was because she didn't want to break the silent treatment she was fixing to give him.

•

The house was spic and span when the young McCartys rolled in that night. Molly didn't utter one word of explanation in hopes that maybe Scott hadn't noticed. And Scott didn't utter a word because he assumed the housekeeper—the young girl he'd seen a few weeks before—had been over to clean up, although he did consider it quite odd that she'd come over on a Saturday night—especially during the Picnic.

Oh well. What do I care what she does on a Saturday night? As long as my wife is happy, I'm happy.

•

At 3:15 a.m. there was absolutely no trace of the El Dorado Springs Picnic. Just like every year, as soon as the clock strikes midnight, the carnival workers begin the arduous task of disassembling all rides and the game booths. The cleaning crew, headed up by Eula Mae Jones (with her eccentric grandson, Sugar, in tow), and the Picnic planning committee are always busy bees picking up every piece of trash and debris scattered throughout the park and along the rock wall. This year the revitalization committee (sans Winthrop who considered himself "too good" for the task and had better things to do) pitched in to sweep away the detritus accumulated up and down Main Street.

All was at it should be when Chief Schierreck did his final inspection. The Parkview Café was his final stop. Owner Joy Scott, who was part of the clean-up crew every year, made it a tradition to host the rest of the team and cook breakfast when they were finished with the cleanup. She invited the chief to sit a spell.

"Sunnyside, scrambled, or over-easy?"

"None for me." He removed his cap, scratched the top of his sweaty scalp, and placed it back on his head. "I'm headed home."

Roland raised his mug and toasted, "Well, here's to another successful Picnic, boys and girls."

"Here! Here!" The small crowd raised their orange juice glasses and in unison began to hoot and holler.

Schierreck shook his head in disbelief, wondering how they could all be so energetic and still going strong when he was about to pass out from exhaustion. Still, he fought the urge to speed home to his nice, comfy bed, and trudged up Spring Street about half a block to check on Ollie.

He heard Ollie's wheezy, raspy breath before he saw him. The sorry old man was stretched out in the back seat, and despite the overwhelming heat, had a wool army-issued blanket pulled tight around his chin, muttering something the chief couldn't quite make out— "Minette" or maybe "Antoinette."

"Hey, buddy, sounds like you're having a dream about the ladies...don't let me interrupt."

The city thermometer read a sultry 97 degrees, not to mention the thick humidity that pushed the heat index up to about 106. People had been passing out right and left from the heat—and not just old folks, either, and here was Ollie wrapped up in that dad-gum blanket. Schierreck flipped on the fan, but it was plum dead. Out of battery.

As Ollie's breath thickened, he contemplated forcing the man to go to the hospital. Instead, he gently took one corner of the blanket and pulled it down to his ankles, leaving only his feet covered. Schierreck decided after he got some shut-eye he'd come back and check on the old man. If he wasn't better then, he'd make him go to the hospital regardless of how much he might protest.

Schierreck then climbed behind the wheel of the squad car, put the pedal to the metal, with nothing on his mind other than stripping down to his birthday suit and losing consciousness between the cool, comforting bed sheets in his air-conditioned double-wide.

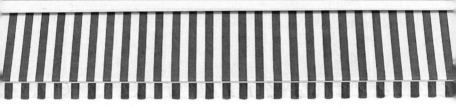

A Shot in the Dark

C haos reigned supreme on what should have been the quietest day of the year. As a matter of fact, the church community hadn't seen this much weeping and gnashing of teeth since the city outlawed snake handling back in 1964 when Ronnie Mack Jones died after being bit by a giant rattler during tent revival.

Eula May was the first one to witness the carnage. Never mind that she'd only had less than three hours of sleep. Since Sugar had a habit of sneaking out of the house and wandering around downtown, she was used to either getting by on very little rest or at least sleeping with one eye open.

Anyway, it was her Sunday to be in charge of communion, and she was up at the crack of dawn loading the unleavened bread, the grape juice, and neatly stacking the rows of tin plates, lining them up and packing them tightly in the floorboard of the back seat so they wouldn't tip over.

Sugar sat himself in the front as Eula May cranked up the radio volume. Eula May was singing along to the bluegrass version of "When We All Get to Heaven" and having a grand old time when Sugar pointed off to the right and muttered the word, "Twenty-five."

His grandmother didn't pay him any mind. She was used to him talking in riddles and saying things that often didn't make a lick of sense.

"Twenty-five," he repeated, gesturing to the left. This time Eula May couldn't help but pay attention.

"What in the…heck?" She stopped herself before she said the "h-e-double toothpicks" word—it just wasn't right to cuss on a Sunday. Her first thought was that some of the carnies had thrown a rock at the window, but as she slowed the car to a crawl and took a closer look, Eula Mae went into hysterics.

Every single, solitary store window had been shot completely out. Glass—small slivers and huge chunks—lay all over the sidewalk and into Main Street. Large shards dangerously dangled from a few of the windows, ready to crash to the pavement at the slightest hint of wind. Dozens of shell casings were scattered everywhere.

Eula May was cursing the fact that she hadn't given in to the concept of a cell phone. Vowing that the first thing tomorrow morning she was going to see Cari Spillman at the Phone Booth, she then burned rubber up Main Street and fish-tailed into the police station parking lot.

By 9:30, there wasn't a saved soul anywhere in town that hadn't heard about the downtown mess.

The "sinners" found out shortly thereafter.

"If you'd been at morning services you'd have known about this earlier and the chief could have questioned you as well," Wilhelmina scolded Molly, who was piping-hot mad about having to replace the café window for the second time in less than two weeks.

"You know I had to take Scott to the airport, Mama. And why would he want to question me? Jennifer is the one to interview since she lives above the restaurant. She had to have heard the gunshots and the glass breaking."

"He did try to interview her, but she wasn't home."

"That's strange," Molly replied. "She usually tells me if she's going somewhere overnight."

"Well, maybe she just wanted to get away for a few days since the café was closed," suggested Wilhelmina.

"And miss the Picnic? No way. She's starved and tanned for two months to get ready for this weekend. She wouldn't miss the opportunity to have somewhere to go show off a skinny, tanned, scantily clad body. In the meantime, I'd like to get my hands on that Roy Bob!"

"The police don't believe it was Roy Bob."

•

"It's not Roy Bob Benson. That we know for sure," Pete Willis, the department's best investigator, tossed a file on the chief's desk. "He hasn't been anywhere near this town—not even the county—in about three weeks."

Chief looked at the file and read Willis's notes.

"For the past month he's been working for a construction company in Bentonville, Arkansas. I talked to the foreman himself."

The chief wasn't convinced. "Bentonville's not that far away. He could have easily come back, waited till the coast was clear, shot everything up, and been back in Arkansas before the crack of dawn."

Pete shook his head.

"According to witnesses he's been onsite for twenty-two days straight—rotating shifts. He not only worked the overnight shift last night, but he also worked the overnight shift the same night The Hillbilly Debutante Café got their little paint job."

The chief was getting a headache. This was supposed to be an easy job, but the past few weeks he'd had to work hard to earn his keep, and he wasn't too happy about it. He was sure that Papula girl was hiding something, but he wasn't for sure what. All he knew was that she'd been very uncooperative when they'd wanted to know where she had been the night before.

Suddenly the chief grabbed his car keys and leapt out of his chair, heading for the door.

"Where you headed?" Pete called after him.

"To question a witness!" And with that, he was off like a dirty shirt, driving ninety-to-nothing out of the parking lot headed straight for downtown.

The End of an Era

Poor Ollie was stiff as a board. The county coroner assured Chief that by all accounts it didn't look like there was any foul play involved—just that old Ollie had plum tuckered out.

"Of course we won't know one hundred percent until we do an autopsy," he said.

"He's been sick the past few times I've seen him," Chief said. "I tried to call the ambulance last week, and he refused. I should've just loaded up the sorry ol' son of a gun and taken him myself."

"Well, nothin' you can do about it now," the coroner replied. "Ollie was a grown man—and *strange,* to say the least, but still he was enough of sound mind to take care of himself."

Chief laughed. "You call *this* taking care of yourself?"

The old car resembled a giant stuffed beer can with smelly, yellowed newspapers piled from floorboard to roof and everything else Ollie had owned crammed into every nook and crevice.

Poor Mo-Ped paced back and forth in the seat where a few hours earlier his master had perished. Animals have way better senses than humans give them credit for. Mo-Ped knew that Ollie was dead and that he was now an orphan cat.

The two men ignored the feline and continued on with their assessment of Ollie, still trying, after all these years, to make sense of why a man would choose to live in his car.

"I know it broke his mama's heart that he wouldn't live with them," the coroner said, slapping the hood of Ollie's car. "They let him stay with them for a bit after he got back from Viet Nam. Lasted for about a month, and that's when he bought this old wreck. They offered to buy him a house, but he flat refused. Said he had money of his own and if he wanted to buy a house, he'd do it. Then he packed up what little bit he had and moved out. Rest is history."

Tired of being ignored, Mo-Ped jumped from the top of the car and landed on all fours onto the street below. He rubbed against the chief's legs several times, but the chief was too engrossed in the coroner's story to bother with the animal.

"The old man just got down-right belligerent after Ollie had been out here for about a week," the coroner continued. "He told him, 'You're embarrassing your mother to no end. She won't leave the house for fear of what the ladies at her garden club are saying. Get yourself together, or I'm going to cut you off without a penny!' But as you can see"—the coroner pointed over his shoulder with his thumb—"that threat didn't do a bit of good."

Speaking of threats, the threat of not knowing where his next meal was coming from was becoming all too real for Mo-Ped.

Me-ow! Ollie had been so sick the past few days that he hadn't been able to care for the cat. It had been that long since Mo-Ped had had anything to eat.

"And sure 'nuff," the coroner proceeded to a completely captivated Chief, "when Old Man Griffin died he left every penny to his wife's beloved garden club. Ollie didn't see a penny."

Chief shook his head, looking around the park, evidence everywhere of Ollie's fathers money put to good use. "We have beautiful trees and flowers, but it's a complete ghost town down here."

"Well now, son, you have to remember it wasn't like that back then." The coroner could remember when El Dorado had a thriving economic community. "And who would have thought it would ever change?"

"Exactly. Who'd have thought?" They were both silent for a few minutes, the coroner lost in memories of the past and Chief suddenly aware of the cat's claws stuck in his left pant leg. He bent over and picked up the cat and then sneezed within two seconds of doing so.

"Ollie have any family left?" he asked, wondering what the heck they were going to do with the car and all the stuff inside.

The coroner shook his head.

"Nope. He was an only child of two only children."

In between sneezing, the chief managed to say, "I'll have someone out here first thing in the morning to clean the car out and haul it away. Also, I'll put a squad car out here tonight to make sure kids don't come around and decide to break in for a souvenir. In the meantime, you wanna cat?"

"Nope, I hate cats."

"I know the feelin'." While Chief's nasal passages were clamping shut and his eyes watering profusely, Mo-Ped purred contentedly.

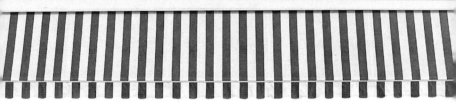

Sugar's Clue

The next morning at The Hillbilly Debutante Café, everyone's eyes were glued on the television that Jennifer had brought in so they could watch Peggy, who now went by the name Summer Stevens. El Dorado had been in the news a lot lately and seemed that Peg...I mean Summer, had more than a hint of a vengeful gleam in her eye when she reported on the current events.

Michael sat brooding at one of the three back tables that were pushed together where members of the revitalization committee were waiting to get the meeting started, waiting, as always, for Kathryn to arrive.

Everyone was speculating on who was responsible for the recent vandalism.

Jerry Ray, today sporting a pixie short red wig, jokingly said to Drex Salazar, "Maybe Chief should question you since you're making a killing replacing all these windows."

Drex stuffed the measuring stick in his back pocket and jotted the measurements on his tablet. "Not funny. And don't expect windows in all the stores to be replaced anytime soon. I'll get the one here, over at

Carl's, and down at the Parkview, but I refuse to replace the buildings that Max Montgomery owns until he pays up front."

Jerry Ray reached into his black Chanel bag and laid a twenty-dollar bill on the table next to his bill. "Ha! I also learned my lesson the hard way with that guy. Let's just say gettin' money from him is like tryin' to get blood from a turnip. I don't fix anything on any of his cars until I get paid first."

And then, of course, the conversation and speculation turned to the inevitable—Ollie—in which Jerry Ray gave his two cents on that as well.

"I'll betcha anything the autopsy reveals he was poisoned or smothered."

"If they wanted to kill him, they would have just shot him," said Eula May in a voice that I thought had a snotty, know-it-all edge to it. Since she was the first one on the scene and to report the vandalism, she seemed to take ownership on the whole story. Actually, if you'll remember, it was Sugar who noticed it first, but you'll never hear Eula May admit that.

"Eula May's right," Anne-Donavan pointed out, much to Eula May's delight (if the smirk on her face was any indication). "It would have been too risky to stop and strangle him—"

"And it would have taken way too long," Jenn piped in as she made the refill rounds with the coffee pot. "Same with poisoning." She used a deep, gruff voice, her interpretation of what a would-be killer might sound like. "Here, Ollie, eat this…or drink this." Pretending to be the culprit, she then tapped her foot as she held up her wrist watch, mockingly counting the minutes until the "poison" took effect.

"See," she said, making her point, "that would just be stupid."

"And who would want to kill Ollie anyway?" Ernie Harris asked. "He was perfectly harmless. Crazy, but harmless."

"Because he could identify whoever was shooting the place up like it was the OK Corral, that's why," stated Anne-Donavan. "And whoever it was had to work fast because even though there aren't any houses too close by, people could still hear the shattering glass and the gunshots."

Michael called across the café, "Jennifer, you live upstairs; you had to have heard the ruckus."

"I wasn't home," Jennifer said nervously then immediately dodged more questions by saying, "I have to go upstairs and check on the cat!"

Just then, the jingle bell on the café door rang as Kathryn entered, apologizing for being late once again.

"Did I just hear you say you had to check on the cat?" Kathryn asked. "When did you get a cat?"

"The chief asked me to take Mo-Ped," Jennifer quickly replied as she slipped behind the door leading to her upstairs apartment.

Eula May, aware that if she didn't take control the conversation would turn away from the important part she'd played, said, "As you know, as it is every single year, I'm always the last one to leave downtown after the Picnic is over, and I told the police I didn't see one dog-gone suspicious thing."

"Twenty-five," muttered Sugar, so low that you almost had to be sitting right next to him to hear it.

"What did you say, buddy?" Brother Jeff asked.

"Twenty-five," Sugar repeated and then stuffed an enormous amount of biscuits and gravy in his mouth, which proceeded to drip down both sides of his chin and onto the white linen napkin lying in his lap.

"Twenty-five what, Sugar?" Jerry Ray asked, but for whatever reason—probably because he'd just stuffed another big spoonful of gravy in his mouth—Sugar was done talking.

Money Honey

B y Thursday morning, downtown El Dorado Springs was good as new. The shattered glass fragments had been cleaned up, shell casings collected as evidence, and thanks to the pressure on Max to pay up, every single window was reinstated. And on the outskirts of town in a small country cemetery, Ollie was laid to rest.

As a small group of us (eleven counting myself) gathered around an open grave to pay our last respects, another small group was in the tedious process of cleaning out Ollie's car.

The musty, discolored newspapers stacked ceiling high were filed in chronological order from 1969 to 1985. For all anyone could figure, he either didn't buy any more after that, or he read them and threw them away. Why he kept them from those particular years was anyone's guess. There were a few books, pictures of his parents, and a high school yearbook dated 1966.

Amidst a new package of toilet paper (just in case you're wondering, the city park has public bathrooms with twenty-four-hour access), was a bar of Dial soap—and $226,348.52.

Let me repeat that: in Ollie's 1969 Thunderbird stuffed in between every nook, cranny, and crevice—even in the hubcaps, there was money—bills—to the tune of $226,348. The fifty-two cents was found under the front passenger seat.

If that's not enough to ruffle your britches, hidden in between clothes that were stuffed in the back windshield were bank books and ledgers. Come to find out, Ollie had money socked away in banks all the way from Tulsa, Oklahoma, to St. Louis, Missouri, to Alexandria, Virginia. All totaled, Ollie's net worth was well over one million dollars.

Where did he get the money? Why would a millionaire live like a pauper—in his *car*, sharing cans of cat food with his cat when he could afford a house? Heck, in this part of the country, he could have owned three houses! These were just a few of the questions that had folks around these parts confounded.

It seems that Ollie Griffin was a man of many secrets.

Ollie's Story

SAIGON, VIET NAM 1968

t's often said "what doesn't kill you only makes you stronger." For the most part, that's true. But sometimes it's not. Some situations may not kill you physically but they can steal your joy and eat away at your very soul. That's exactly what happened to Oliver Nathaniel Griffin.

The summer after his senior year, his plans of playing the lead in *Romeo and Juliet* at the Kansas City Opera and later attending the University of Missouri were put on hold when Uncle Sam called him to serve. A few weeks later like many young men of his age, he was shipped off to war in a far-off place called Viet Nam.

Early on, the army had recognized two important qualities in Private Giffin. First, his ability to handle a rifle; and second, his maturity level compared to the other young men surrounding him. I suppose his musical training taught him discipline, although in our small town, I think a lot of people unfairly questioned his masculinity. Ollie would need to cash in on that discipline and maturity to complete the difficult tasks he would be assigned to do.

After a few months of intense training, according to his first sergeant, Ollie exhibited amazing capabilities with a Winchester 700. Bragging to his superiors that Private Griffin could "hit a flea on a hummingbird's butt at least a thousand yards away," Ollie was whisked away to a private and remote part of the jungle about twenty miles outside of Saigon. His first mission? To assassinate a Viet Cong colonel who had once been loyal to the United States and now was the brains behind the North Vietnamese arms shipments to the south.

Ollie's training kicked in immediately. He didn't hesitate for a second to pull the trigger when the intended target stepped out of his cabin into the heavy, humid air. Just as the enemy raised a lit match to his cigar, the bullet from Ollie's rifle caught him right between the eyes. Very calmly, Ollie hiked through the jungle back to camp. There was no time for him to contemplate what he'd just done. He was immediately choppered off to another assignment just like this one. And then another and another. Sweet, sensitive Ollie, it seems, was a natural-born killer.

Ollie was staying strong, focused, although it wasn't easy to go from being a sheltered, small town boy to an assassin—killing people he didn't even know on command. Luckily, he'd had just enough time in-between missions to fall head over heels in love, which played a huge part in keeping him sane.

Minh Nyet was the most beautiful girl he'd ever laid eyes on. Sure, there were pretty girls back in El Dorado

Springs, but none of them had ever given him the time of day—not that he'd tried, mind you. Ollie was painfully shy. The only time he had felt comfortable in his own skin was when he was on stage singing.

But being an opera singer in a town where country is the music of choice…well, let's just say girls weren't exactly waiting in line to snag a date with Ollie. And he wouldn't have dreamed of approaching a girl back home. But with Minh Nyet, everything was just so easy.

She had caught him staring at her at the market. She smiled, ducked her head coquettishly and paid for her purchases. Feeling uncharacteristically confident, he approached her and offered to carry them. Six blocks and three hours later he knew everything about her – and he loved her anyway.

You see, Minh Nyet was a prostitute. Like many other young women in her country, she just did what she had to do to survive. Ollie understood this. He would do no more than kiss her; not because he was ashamed of her, but because when they did make love, he wanted it to be special. He would rescue her from this godforsaken place, marry her, and when *it* happened, it would be for love and he would be her one and only. She would never be forced to do such despicable things again.

Ollie saved every single penny he earned from his army paycheck. For mealtimes he ate at the mess hall. He never partied or hung out at the bars with the guys. Not a dime was wasted on anything other than necessities. He and Minh Nyet were going to be married, and he had a special savings account that would allow them to build their dream home.

Every spare moment Ollie and Minh Nyet had was spent making plans for their future in America. They would draw house plans, adding bedrooms for each of their future children, whom they'd already named.

Never were two people more in love. While it was the dream of most Vietnamese girls to attach themselves to the first American soldier and head for greener pastures, this wasn't the case with Minh Nyet. She loved Ollie more than life itself. She couldn't wait to be his wife and spend her life trying to make him the happiest man in the world.

He couldn't wait to get her out of this hellhole, take her home, and show her what it was like to be *really* loved, not used and then tossed away. Within fifteen months of being in Viet Nam and doing back to back missions, Ollie was offered a furlough.

"This is my last mission for a while," he promised Minh Nyet. "As soon as I'm finished, we'll go back to the United States and get married. I'll have just enough leave time to find you a small apartment. I'll have to come back here for one more mission, which will probably take about three months, and then I'll be back home for good."

He hadn't told his parents about her. Not yet. He wanted to wait until he could introduce them in person. His mother would want Minh Nyet to stay with them until he could come home permanently, but he wanted Minh Nyet to have her privacy. His mother could be over-bearing and besides, after sharing a home with fifteen other girls, she deserved a home of her own.

"I'd like to save for a few more years," Ollie explained. "That way we'll have a bigger down payment. So if you can handle living in a small apartment for a while…"

Minh Nyet nestled her head on his shoulder, feeling so safe in his arms. "I don't care where I live," she said. "I don't even care if we ever have that house, Ollie. My home and my heart are wherever you are. I cannot wait to be your wife."

"Oh no." Ollie wrapped his arms around her and kissed the top of her head. "We *will* have that house. It will be ours, and no one can ever take it from us. And it will be beautiful—just like you."

•

This mission was a little different. Ollie would not be working alone. The chopper ride was longer than usual, and it dropped him off at a landing zone that nobody in America would admit even existed. There he met his partners simply known as Delta and Charlie. Ollie's code name was Baker. Each man was instructed to not divulge their true names or ask any personal questions of the other. After the mission was completed, they would each go to their assigned places, wait for their respective choppers, and never see each other again.

After two days of hiking through the jungle hills, they reached the peak along the mountain that was to become home. There were several trees with larger than usual limbs—big enough for a grown man to sit semi-comfortably. Each one took a limb and sat quietly, waiting, watching.

Their view was perfect. The target was a Russian technician that they guessed was a spy of some sort. According to their superiors, he was helping the Viet Cong, and his picture had made it to the powers that be in Washington.

A full day passed while the three sat silently, cramped, afraid to change to a more comfortable position for fear of making noise. There was still no sign of the Russian. Once during the day, a small troop of North Vietnamese regulars on patrol had passed directly beneath them. Ollie and his partners, fully camouflaged, remained motionless for what seemed like hours, while one smoked a cigarette directly under the branch that Ollie was perched on. Ollie wished now that they had a better spot. He wished they weren't up the tree since it would take too long to get down once the shot was fired. He felt exposed; something didn't seem right.

Then things started happening out of order. A thump and two rifle's sounds were heard—one was his, but the other was far away. They'd been spotted! He looked over at Charlie just in time to see his helmet fly off his head. Delta fell to the ground forty feet below, and now Ollie was scanning the opposite hill looking for that glint. He saw it and again saw the trail of the bullet, and this time it was headed straight toward him. As his world faded to black, Minh Nyet's face was the last thing he remembered.

•

"Good morning, Private."

Ollie blinked his eyes a few times and tried to keep them open, but it was no use. Not only did the sunlight peeping through the blinds hurt his eyes, but he was so weak he didn't have the strength to focus.

"Where am I?" he asked. His throat was parched and he tried to swallow, but it was painful.

"You're in the hospital recovering from a gunshot wound to the chest," she replied as she changed his IV bag. "It barely missed your heart. You're a lucky young man."

He didn't feel lucky. He was sore and it hurt to breathe. "How long have I been here?"

"Three weeks today."

Three weeks? He had to get to Minh Nyet. Ignoring his pain, he immediately pushed himself up with his elbows and tried to throw his leg over the side of the bed.

"Hold on, soldier." The nurse gently pushed him back to the bed, and he was so weak he couldn't fight it. "You are in no shape to be getting out of this bed. I appreciate your enthusiasm, but it's going to be at least another week before you can travel, and then you'll get a one-way ticket back to the States."

Without argument, he laid his head back down on the pillow and although he tried to fight it he fell back asleep and didn't wake up for another three days. Feeling significantly stronger, and confident the nurse was pre-occupied, Ollie removed the IV and tubes from his arms. Stealing clothes from a soldier in the next bed, he left the hospital through a back door just as the place became chaotic when a new surge of incoming wounded had distracted the staff.

When he got about a block and a half from the hospital, he whistled at a young rickshaw driver to carry him the next several blocks to where Minh Nyet lived.

The sweat streaming down Ollie's face had nothing to do with the stifling heat nor the pain he felt with every step of the rickshaw driver. The anxiety he was feeling was a mixture of two things: fear that Minh Nyet might think he had abandoned her, and fear because he'd heard the nurses talking about the fatal bombings that had happened in the city the past few days.

He'd hoped it wasn't true. He'd prayed it wasn't. But as he got closer to Minh Nyet's neighborhood, he saw the awful devastation.

The destruction was massive. The air reeked of death and decay. The area was so unrecognizable that Ollie wasn't even sure if he was in the right place until he saw a familiar form amidst the rubble. It was one of the girls who lived in Minh Nyet's house. He didn't know her name, but he'd seen her several times over the past year when he'd come to call on his beloved.

"Minh Nyet!" Ollie cried out, his eyes searching everywhere. Men and women were digging through the rubble trying to salvage what they could, some looking for food, others for loved ones. Children roamed the streets, some crying as they searched for their mothers, others still in silent shock.

"She is gone," said the girl, staring straight ahead.

"Where is she?" he asked. He was weak and could hardly stand, but he willed himself to keep going.

"Where is she?" he was now screaming.

The young girl started to cry. "She is dead." She then looked up at him, tears now falling, leaving clean lines down her dust-covered face. "I am the only one left. Everyone is dead."

"No!" shouted Ollie. "No!"

He furiously started digging through the rubble, grabbing chunks of concrete, dirt, and debris. He worked for hours until his hands were raw and bloody. He had to stop a few times to catch his breath, and then with all the strength he could muster he'd start rummaging again. He found the bodies of several of the other girls, as well as a couple of American soldiers before he found Minh Nyet. With the exception of a trickle of dried blood around her nose and a deep gash in her skull, she looked perfect, as though she were sleeping.

Her lower body remained buried under the crushed brick; he cradled her upper body next to his. He rocked back and forth, running his fingers through her silky black hair, his tears falling like raindrops.

"Oh God, please no…please, please, please no…"

•

A few weeks later Ollie was discharged and sent back home. He holed up at Betty Sue and Earl's place just long enough for his wound to completely heal—at least his physical wound. If Post Traumatic Stress Syndrome had a name back then, folks probably would've blamed Ollie's moving into the Thunderbird on that.

Instead, they thought he had just gone cuckoo. If only they had known how bad he was hurting, how broken he was. But they couldn't know because he never told them—not even Betty Sue and Earl. He couldn't imagine ever living in a house without Minh Nyet. So he didn't.

With the exception of what he needed to just barely get by, he never spent a dime. The money he'd put away for Minh Nyet's dream home accrued interest year after year, making him a millionaire, and the money he received from his disability check was cashed and stashed, which explains the money the clean-up crew found throughout his car.

What they wouldn't find was his Purple Heart. It had found its way into the trash decades earlier. Ollie saw no significance in keeping it. He didn't see himself as brave. He was just doing his job—a job he entered into blindly, never asking questions. But he'd paid for it. Oh Lord, how he'd paid. Every single night, as he drifted into fitful slumber and came face-to-face with the ghosts, the distorted, bloody faces of the men he'd killed, he knew within a shadow of a doubt, that Minh Nyet's death was his payback.

Back to Normal—
Or not

For a while life in El Dorado Springs was back to normal—even better than normal. Since Ollie had no family, he left his money to the revitalization committee to be dispersed to prospective business owners—with strict stipulations, of course. Number one: new-fangled fancy showers were to be added to the park restrooms, and number two: a big donation was to be made to the El Dorado Springs Garden Club in memory of Ollie's mama, Betty Sue Griffin.

A few took advantage of the money. Drex Salazar expanded Dash Glass Replacement and Installation to include floor covering as well. And the Allison brothers—Greg, Davin, and Troy—decided to branch out from their tire shop on Highway 54 and bought the old opera house on Main Street right next door to The Hillbilly Debutante Café. Now it's a movie theatre, and once a month they shut the camera off and the stage comes to life with a country music variety show, showcasing the talents of our local singers. It's always on a Thursday night so as not to compete with Ronnie Swopes's Saturday night hoedown at his Circle S Feed Store. (You wouldn't find that kind of conviviality going on in the big city now, would you?)

As for the revitalization committee, they invested in beautiful street lighting reminiscent of what the city had back at the turn of the century. They've also used some of the money to advertise in other cities and out of state to try to lure business owners to our wonderful community. They are taking baby steps, but every step counts.

Yes, everything *was* pretty much back to normal, but as the old saying goes, "all good things must end."

Revelations

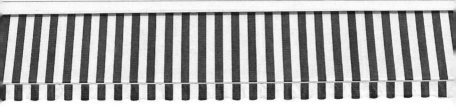

"Hello!" Molly answered the phone, and not very nicely, I might add. You know it's going to be a bad day when your cell phone rings at 3:30 am, your best friend is on the line and she's a blubbering mess.

"Mo-Ped is gone!" Jennifer was hysterical.

"He's a cat, Jenn. Cats always run away and don't come back til they're darn good and ready."

She's calling me this early in the morning over a missing cat? She's only had him for a week and a half. She can't be that attached to him.

"No! He's dead! Someone murdered him, and they left him by the café door! You've got to come down here quick!"

•

The police cars, flashing lights, and a small crowd of investigators lead by the police chief was becoming a way-too-familiar scene to Molly. Sugar Jones was on one of his late-night-early-morning-can't-sleep jaunts through town and parked his butt on the café entry steps silently watching the melee.

"Sug, does your mama know where you're at?" Molly asked him and then said to Schierreck, "Did you try to question him? He had to have seen something."

The chief shook his head in frustration. "He's absolutely no help at all. When we try to ask him if he saw anything, he just keeps saying 'twenty-five' over and over."

He opened his notebook and showed her a crumply piece of paper with newspaper cutouts of different sizes forming the words "you're next."

"This was found next to the cat."

Molly read it and tried to take it for a closer look, but Schierreck drew it back.

"We're still testing it for finger prints," he said, slipping it back into a manila folder.

"What happened to the cat, anyway?"

"It looks like he was hit over the head with a blunt object. I don't think that's what did him in though. I'm guessing it just stunned him long enough for whoever did it to asphyxiate him. There was a plastic bag tied around his head."

Molly felt sick to her stomach.

"Good grief—who *does* that?"

"Twenty-five," muttered Sugar, but as usual no one was listening.

"You're a senator's wife, Molly. We are going to have to let the feds know about this so they can assign a security detail for you," Schierreck ordered.

"No! Absolutely not!" Molly protested loud enough that the investigators and Jennifer turned to see what was going on. She lowered her voice to a whisper, "Don't you *dare* get the feds involved in this! If Scott gets wind of this, he'll have me back in DC so fast my head will spin. I am *begging* you to just handle this on your own."

The chief's long silence put the fear of God into Molly.

"Besides, we don't even know if that note was meant for me!" she argued.

Schierreck answered, "I'll let it go this time, Molly, but just this time. If I hear of anything else, I'm calling the feds, and you're having a bodyguard till we catch this person. End of argument."

"Fair enough." She breathed a collective sigh of relief. He would have a fit if he knew about all of the dead calls she'd been getting. Not to mention the fact that someone was figuring a way to get into the house without breaking a lock or a window.

Schierreck reached for the small notebook in his back pocket.

"Now I'm going to go question your buddy over there. I can't get a straight answer from her on how she found the cat any more than I can on her whereabouts a few Saturday nights ago when the windows were all shot out."

"Come on, Chief. You surely don't suspect Jennifer!"

"I've known Jennifer my whole life so no. *But…*"

"But?"

"You know how Jennifer's always getting mixed up with the wrong guy. Well, what if she's in over her head this time? What is she's involved with Roy Bob's partner?"

Considering Jenn's past history for dating losers, Molly couldn't exactly argue.

•

"You're beginning to sound like the chief!" Jennifer slammed the coffee pot on the counter. "Do you think I had something to do with this crap that's been going on around here the past month?"

She was in the midst of starting a few pots for the breakfast crowd, as it was already 6:35—only twenty-five minutes away from opening time.

"Don't be ridiculous, Jenn. I'm just worried about you. You've been acting all sneaky-like lately—it's like you're hiding something. The chief thinks you might be involved with someone who's in charge of all the helter-skelter that's been going on and that you might be in danger. I'm starting to wonder the same thing."

"It's nobody's business what I do or who I do it with!"

"Whoever this person is just killed a cat, Jennifer! A living, breathing animal. So if you have any suspicions that this person you're seeing is—"

"Winthrop! I'm seeing Winthrop Worthington! I've been all 'sneaky-like' as you put it because we don't want anyone to know until *after* he's filed for divorce."

This revelation rendered Molly speechless—but only for a second. "Have you lost your ever-lovin' mind? Jennifer, seriously! Winthrop? What are you thinking?"

"I am not having this conversation with you right now!" Jennifer made a mad dash through the door, running smack-dab into Rosemary, who dropped her purse, scattering the contents all over the floor.

"What's wrong with her?" Rosemary asked, annoyed that Jennifer hadn't even said as much as "sorry" for almost knocking her down. "And what's all that red stuff all over the sidewalk? Looks like blood."

"It's a long story," Molly replied as she dropped to her knees and helped the woman pick up her belongings. There was a small packet of tissues, a half pack of gum, and a tube of pink lipstick, which surprised Molly; she'd never seen Rosemary wear any kind of cosmetic.

"I can't find my bill fold," Rosemary said, on the verge of panic. "I have to have my billfold!"

The usually patient Molly was in no mood for one of Rosemary's mini-nervous breakdowns today. Lord knows she was on the brink of one herself, and it wasn't even seven o'clock. And since Jennifer was off on one of her own and she was stuck running The Hillbilly Debutante Café, there would be no time for one anytime soon.

"Here it is, Rosemary. It's under this chair."

Molly let go of the billfold, thinking that Rosemary had a good grip on it, but once again it hit the floor with a plop, sending coins rolling under booths and a few pictures sliding across the floor.

"Oh, Rosemary, I'm so sorry. I'm so nervous this morning. I guess I've just got butter fingers." She picked up a quarter and two nickels and a small picture lying nearby. Picking up the photo, she looked at it and immediately recognized the young girl smiling back at her.

"I know this girl!" Molly *almost* said as she handed the picture to Rosemary. It was the blonde girl who always wore white flowing clothes and several times a week was seen standing at the fence with the horses and had even been caught a few times inside the paddock with them. And, although Molly didn't know it, it was also the same girl Scott had seen peering down from his office window.

But before Molly could ask how Rosemary knew the girl, Rosemary took the picture, held it close to her heart and in a sad, almost inaudible voice said, "That's my Ashley."

"*Who?*" Molly was stunned. She could have sworn that Rosemary just said the girl in that photo—the girl that Molly had seen on her property over a dozen times—was her dead daughter.

Rosemary gently touched the picture with her slender fingers.

"It's Ashley, my daughter," she smiled slightly, her eyes still glued to the photo. She slowly sat down and at one of the tables and then looked at Molly, "I'm sure your mother has told you about her."

Molly sat down across from her, trying to keep her composure.

"No, actually Mama hasn't done a good job of keeping me up to date on things." She reached across and squeezed Rosemary's hand. "I'd love to hear about her, if you don't mind talking about her, that is."

Rosemary's usually panicky-on-the-brink-of-tears-expression instantly changed to a smile.

"She was such a good girl. Even as a baby she was such a delight. She almost never cried. And oh my! From the time she could walk she had to have everything neat and orderly. I never really had to do a thing around the house 'cause she was always going through cleaning, straightening things up. I'd do housework and always come back and find it redone because it didn't measure up to Ashley's standards."

"Keep going," Molly said, glancing over Rosemary's shoulder at the clock. "We've got a few more minutes til we open, and I'm going to pour us a cup of coffee. Cream, no sugar, right?"

"Yes, please," replied Rosemary. She didn't speak again until she got her coffee. She took a swallow and then continued.

"We home-schooled Ashley, you know," Rosemary searched Molly's face for judgment, but there was none. "Folks thought we were being too old-fashioned, wanting to shelter her from the rest of the world. But home-schooling was what *she* wanted. We sent her to school in town til she was in third grade and finally we just gave in to her belly-achin' and sure enough, I home-schooled her."

"Was she being bullied at school?" Molly wondered.

Rosemary laughed out loud, a sweet sound. "Oh my goodness, no! Ashley may have been a tiny bit of a thing—and she looked as frail as a porcelain doll—but she was very strong-willed and she never let anyone get the best of her. Besides, everyone loved Ashley and she loved them."

She paused and took another drink of her coffee. "But what Ashley loved more than anything was that farm. Every inch of it—the cattle, the horses—*especially* the horses. She was the one who named it 'Serenity Farm.' It was her second-grade year, and she had read the word in one of her reading books—she was always reading—and she asked me what it meant. We looked it up in the dictionary. *'Calm, peaceful, untroubled.'* I thought that would be the end of it, but she looked at me and said, 'that's the way this place is, Mama. Calm, peaceful, and untroubled. Do you think Daddy would let us name it Serenity Farm?"

Rosemary laughed again, "David never could say no to her, so the next thing you know he carved out a sign that said 'Serenity Farm,' and welded a fancy wrought-iron post to hang it from."

Now it was Rosemary's turn to look at the clock. Five minutes to opening time. She finished off the last bit of coffee left in her cup, took it over to the kitchen sink, and reached for one of the aprons hanging from a rack behind the bar.

"Rosemary, can I ask you…what happened to Ashley?" Molly was afraid to upset Rosemary right before opening time. She needed the woman to have her wits about her, especially since it looked as if it were just going to be the two of them waitressing. Molly seriously doubted that Jennifer was coming back today.

Oddly enough, Rosemary was fine. No one ever seemed to want to talk about Ashley. Even David couldn't bring himself to speak of her. Sometimes it was as if she never existed. She was loving this opportunity.

"It was a riding accident. Once a week she'd take one of the horses and ride a ten-mile stretch. It's a country road, and hardly anyone travels it except for the postal carrier. He popped over the hill and well.... The horse had to be put down immediately. Ashley was fine. A few scrapes on the side of her face. The ambulance crew brought her in to the ER, the doctor looked her over, said she was fine. She'd been wearing a helmet, after all."

Rosemary stopped, and Molly thought that was the end of the conversation. She had so many questions her head was spinning, but she was afraid to press Rosemary further, and she sure as heck couldn't tell her that she thought Ashley was still there! Molly herself couldn't wrap her head around that! There had to be another explanation, but she sure didn't know what it would be.

"Everything seemed fine," Rosemary continued. "She was quiet that night and went to bed early—I mean *really* early—like 6:30. We didn't think anything of it. My goodness, it had been such a horrible day. She was upset about the horse....The next morning she didn't get up, and I went in to check on her and she was...gone. They told us later it was a brain hemorrhage ...if she hadn't been wearing the helmet she'd probably have died instantly, instead...it just gave us a bit more time with her."

Neither Molly nor Rosemary wanted this conversation to end, but it was now 6:57.

"Molly, it just does my heart good to know you love 'Serenity' like we did—like *Ashley* did.

Every single night she'd pray…"

Rosemary paused for a moment to wipe a tear, and Molly found herself doing the same thing.

"She'd say, 'God, please bless El Dorado Springs and Serenity Farm. Please let me stay here forever.'" Rosemary paused for a moment. Then she looked at Molly and said, "Losing Ashley really rocked my faith."

Molly wanted to offer words of comfort, but she had none.

"I know nothing is forever," Rosemary said. "But she was only seventeen, Molly. I will never understand why He didn't give her more time."

He did, Molly thought, but she knew she could never tell that to Rosemary.

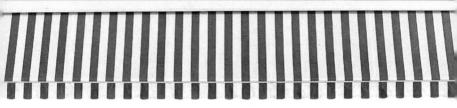

Undercover

So, if the dead cat, the argument with Jenn, and the new revelation that Molly's mysterious housekeeper was a ghost didn't ruin her day, then the guy in the corner that she recognized as an undercover agent from when Scott worked for Senator Bond most definitely sealed the deal.

Chief Schierreck had changed his mind and called the feds anyway. Now Scott would surely demand she move with him to DC. She sighed and rubbed her temples. She looked at her watch. Still a few hours away from that nervous breakdown she so desperately needed.

"I've been watching you all morning, and I have one question." It was Jerry Ray, and he was wearing a pink cowboy hat with his monogram carved out in Swarovski crystals with matching dangling earrings. "Who peed in your cereal?"

"Good grief, Jerry Ray! It's a bit early for all that sparkle, dontcha think?"

"Don't change the subject." He rested his chin ever so gingerly in the cup of his hand so as not to mess up his makeup. "I'm all ears—spill your guts."

"What makes you think something is wrong?" Molly's voice was a whole octave higher, which was a sure sign something was indeed wrong.

"Just women's intuition, I suppose." Jerry Ray smiled.

"Funny."

"Foods up!" hollered Ida as she threw a plate of steaming, over-easy eggs, hash-browns, and toast onto the kitchen window, slamming her hand on the bell, which definitely contributed to Molly's raging headache.

"Ah, saved by the bell!" Molly said over her shoulder as she balanced the plate in one hand and the coffee pot in the other.

"Hey, these are over-easy," Roland Thurman complained as Molly set the hot plate down in front of him. "I ordered sunny-side up."

"And where's my coffee?" Ernie Harris raised his empty cup high in the air. He'd finished his first cup in practically one big swallow and waited patiently for Molly to bring the coffee pot back around for refills, but she had never produced and now his patience was wearing thin.

"I ordered my biscuits and gravy 'bout an hour ago," grumbled another customer.

"All I want is an order of bacon," said another. "Didn't know I'd have to wait till you killed the hog to get it!"

"Patience, everyone!" Molly pleaded as she went around the café refilling coffee. "We're a little short-handed today, as you can see."

"Where's Jennifer, and when is she coming back?" Ernie asked.

Roland agreed, "Yeah, we never have to wait like this when she's around. When is she coming back?"

As Molly pondered the answer to that question herself, in strutted Winthrop, sporting a snazzy pair of expensive sunglasses and his signature "I know something you don't know" grin. Max Montgomery waved at him from across the room and offered him a chair. Less than one minute later, Michael Dailey came trudging through.

"Great," Molly whispered under her breath. Were they here trying to vie for the dead cat story or simply sent from Satan to make her life even more miserable this morning?

Chief Schierreck had promised not to leak the information for a while, but he'd also promised to not put a security detail on her, and now the undercover fed in the corner who had been pretending to read the same page of the newspaper for the past hour was demanding more coffee.

Rosemary pinned a ticket on the roundabout for Ida. "This ticket is circled because it's Anne-Donavan's, and you know she only likes just a pat of butter on her toast."

Ida herself was feeling the tension of the day as well.

"This is not Burger King," she snapped. "Our motto is not 'have it your way.'"

"Rosemary, you take Winthrop and Max's table, and I'll get Michael." Molly was so furious at Winthrop right now she couldn't guarantee she could restrain herself if she went within a foot of him with a pot of hot coffee or a pitcher of ice-cold water or even her bare hands! Jennifer may have picked losers, but to Molly's knowledge she had never dated a married man before, and she would bet the farm that Winthrop had made the first move and pushed and pushed till he'd got what he wanted.

As she got to thinking, she wondered if maybe Winthrop was Roy Bob's partner. Had he been the one behind the strip club? It would make perfect sense. He had the means, and he was slimy enough, that's for sure. Yes, he'd built protest signs and marched just like everyone else, but what better way to throw the attention away from him than to pretend he was against it?

But then again, maybe it was Max Montgomery. He'd been her main suspect for a while, but according to Chief Schierreck, Max was almost broke. The downward spiraling economy and the fact that he had all these empty downtown buildings with no income had supposedly dealt him a huge blow. But wouldn't shooting out the windows enable him to file an insurance claim and keep some of the money?

The two were deep in conversation, both oblivious to Molly's seething glare.

I'll bet the strip club was Max's little project, Winthrop was funding it, and they used Roy Bob as their decoy! She fumbled under the counter for her cell phone and walked like a bat out of you-know-where out the front door to call the chief.

"Undercover Man" quickly put down the newspaper and started to get out of his chair to follow her out.

"Just sit back down!" Molly snapped. "I'm a big girl, and I don't need a babysitter."

He wasn't used to taking orders from a five foot one, one hundred-pound woman, but he was confident that she wasn't getting too far so he sat back down and watched her angrily punch numbers into the keypad.

"Molly, you need to stay out of this," Schierreck scolded her after patiently listening to her theory. "My investigators and I are on top of this, and I don't need you getting involved and botching it up—or worse, getting yourself hurt."

"You know that's not going to happen because you went against your word and had a detail assigned to me anyway!"

"I'm sorry," he apologized. "I got to thinking about it and changed my mind. I couldn't live with myself if something happened to you. Hopefully we'll have this solved soon and everyone can sleep better."

"Fine. I'll stay out of it," she said, both she and Schierreck knowing full well she couldn't have "stayed out of it" if her life depended on it.

Twenty-Five

At 4:48, Brother Jeff was the only customer in the café. Molly sent the ladies home early, offering to clean up and give them a break since it had been such a rough day, but mostly she wanted a few minutes alone with the minister to talk about the main subject that had been weighing heavy on her mind since early that morning—even more so than poor Mo-Ped.

"Can I ask you a weird question?"

With a mouthful of peanut butter pie, he nodded yes and gave a thumbs-up. "Ask me anything you want," he spoke after swallowing. He took a drink of his now-lukewarm coffee and said, "Trust me, I've heard it all."

Molly sure hoped so.

"What happens when we die? Do we go straight to heaven or hell, or do we sleep... I mean, is it possible that our soul could...um...linger for a while?"

"Are you asking me if I believe in ghosts?" Jeff asked before he popped the last bite of pie into his mouth.

"Do you?"

"I'm not saying I do. But then again, I'm not saying I *don't* either. I've just never had an experience with anything in the paranormal realm. Why do you ask?"

Molly contemplated telling him everything then decided against it. "It's just this book I've been reading," she lied. "It's really got me thinking."

"You know, we used to debate this back in preaching school. It could get pretty heated, too. Some would argue that we just go into a sleep—a resting period, if you will—until the Lord comes back. Others argue the purgatory/paradise theory. And then some folks believe that if an accident happens and a person dies suddenly, that sometimes it takes a while for the soul to realize they're dead."

"What do you believe?" Molly was about to bust a gut waiting for his answer. "I mean, don't you think that kind of makes sense?"

"Honestly, Molly, I don't waste a lot of time on it. I try to teach that we need to live our everyday lives in such a way that we don't have to worry about what happens when we pass." He stood up, placed a five-dollar bill on the counter, and said, "Because regardless of what happens, life is for the living."

Easy for you to say, Molly thought as she handed his money back to him. "This one's on the house."

By the time Molly cleaned all the tables, swept and mopped the floors, scrubbed the whole kitchen, and counted the money, it was almost dark. Undercover Man kept his distance, but he did follow her home in his black Lincoln Town Car and parked a little ways down the road to keep an eye on things. Trouble was, he was dead tired due to the fact that he'd driven to El Dorado Springs from Jefferson City before the crack of dawn—an almost three-hour drive—so he was asleep within minutes of cutting the engine.

Sally and Violet eagerly greeted Molly at the door, as well as the smell of freshly brewed coffee. She timidly opened the door and stepped inside.

You couldn't call what she was feeling at that moment *fear*—more like its distant cousin *apprehension*.

"Hello?" Silence.

Her bed had been neatly made, and the bedclothes she'd dropped on the floor in a rush over twelve hours ago were now folded and lay in a neat pile in the white wicker rocking chair next to the bed.

"...*she had to have everything neat and orderly*," Rosemary had said.

"Thank you," Molly called out, but again there was no answer. She waited for...*something*. She wanted the girl to appear—to speak—or give some kind of sign to let Molly know she was present. But nothing.

The dogs were now lying comfortably on the cool kitchen tile. She'd left both of them cooped up inside while she'd rushed in to the café that morning. They should be starving, and they didn't stumble all over themselves trying to get out and relieve themselves when she came home.

Ashley.

"You two have known it all along, haven't you?"

Molly poured herself a cup of coffee.

"....*she asked if she could stay forever...*"

Suddenly, it dawned on Molly that she was privileged. Here she was living in a home, on a farm that a young girl had loved so much that even death hadn't seemed to separate her from it. Now Molly realized that the things that had happened since she moved in were blessings, really—*approval*—and she felt honored.

She also felt exhausted. She drew a hot bath, hoping she could soak away the stress of the day. Heck, not just the stress of the *day*, but the stress of the past few weeks.

The mystery of who had been coming in her house was now solved, and yes it would take a while to get used to it. She wouldn't tell anyone—probably not even Scott. But right now there was an even bigger mystery to solve. Who was trying to destroy their community? And what was their motive?

"Who is doing this? Who? Who? Who?" Molly balled her hands in a fist and punched the water in frustration, splashing it everywhere. The dogs looked at her like she was crazy.

"Ashley…do you know who's been doing this? Can you give me some kind of sign?"

Silence.

"*Someone* had to have seen *something*," she spoke aloud to herself since obviously Ashley wasn't going to communicate.

There were only two people who could have possibly seen something. One was six feet under, and the other wasn't saying anything except the ridiculous phrase, "Twenty-five."

"What the heck does that mean, anyway? Twenty-five?" she asked out loud, grabbing for the thick, fluffy, white towel lying beside the bathtub.

Sally sat beside her, ears pricked up.

"Twenty-five *what*? Twenty-five bullets? Twenty-five minutes? Twenty-five steps?" What did twenty-five represent to Sugar?

"Okay." She threw on a leftover "Scott McCarty for Senate" shirt. "This is a guy who thinks in riddles and numbers, numbers and riddles. After all, he memorizes the whole phone book. So, if I was Sugar, what would be going through my mind?"

In Sugar-style, Molly repeated the number twenty-five to herself over and over. Sally and Violet sat by side and watched her pace back and forth. Then, suddenly it was as if a light bulb came on.

"Oh! My! Gosh! I know who did this!"

64744—the zip code for El Dorado Springs—was Mayor Roland Thurman's vanity license plate on his raspberry red Chrysler LeBaron convertible. Add the numbers 64744, and it equals none other than twenty-five. Sugar, in the only way he knew how, had been trying to tell them all along, and they weren't listening!

But why? Right now that didn't matter. She had to call Schierreck!

She grabbed the phone next to the bedside. The line was dead. *Dang!* She tapped the receiver three or four times, but it was no use. Too excited to stop and be suspicious about just why the phone line might be dead, she grabbed her purse and dumped the contents on the bed. Where was her cell phone? She reached for the pants she was wearing earlier and pulled the pockets inside out. Empty!

"Crap! I left it in the truck!" Furiously yanking a pair of dirty sweatpants out of the clothes hamper, she took one leap and both legs, just like a choreographed dance, slipped through.

She ran out the front door and swiped the phone sitting in the middle of the seat of the old truck. She dialed Schierreck's number, but on the first ring she felt something sharp on the small of her back. She dropped the cell, slowly turned around, and stared straight into the eyes of Roland Thurman.

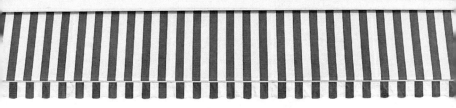

Trapped!

Molly could feel the sharp blade of the knife through her heavy sweatshirt.

"You couldn't leave well enough alone, could you, girl?" His breath was heavy, smelled of liquor, and the cold, evil grin on his face left no doubt that he would push the knife right through her if she made any quick moves.

Inside the house, Sally was going crazy, growling and barking so furiously that Molly thought she would surely jump through the window.

Molly's eyes darted right and then left. *Where is that undercover cop? What to do? What to do?* She tried not to panic. *Talk to him!*

"Roland, why? You're the *mayor*, for goodness sake!"

"I know I'm the mayor, dad-gum it! I've been the mayor for the past twenty-five years, and I'm tired of it!" He was so angry, his face was distorted and his eyes looked as if they'd pop out of their sockets.

"Then why not just retire? Why resort to vandalism and crime?" Molly tried to control her voice, to not show any fear, but she was sweating like crazy, and it wasn't from the ninety-degree weather.

"Because what I *wanted* was to be governor!"

Molly almost laughed. "Roland, please! Who on earth would vote for a strip-club owner for governor? This is the Bible belt!"

Wrong thing to say—he jabbed the knife closer. It hurt, but she remained calm.

"I was a silent partner, you stupid girl! Benson was going to run it, and I was going to share the profits and use it for my campaign fund. Then, when the race got going, I was going to swoop in and shut the place down…"

Now the whole crazy setup was making sense. "You were going to come in and save the day…be the hero," Molly finished for him. "And you think that would have won you the election…"

"It would have worked if you and those idiot parents of yours hadn't stepped in! Your daddy throws his money around like he's God, and—"

Without warning, Molly's knee popped up, and she kicked him in the groin with all her might. While he doubled over in agony, she kicked the knife out of his hand, picked it up off the ground, and ran for dear life for the house. Roland was still screaming, but his anger outweighed his pain, and he grabbed her foot, dragging her to the ground. Molly dropped the knife, he picked it up, and they both got to their feet at the same time. Now he stood between her and the house, where Sally was still jumping and barking so crazy that she surely would've eaten Roland alive if she could have just gotten to him. But Molly knew there was no way she'd make it to the house.

She was sure she could outrun him, so she took off like lightning toward the stable. Roland was a lot older, that's for sure, but she underestimated his stamina. She just barely beat him to the barn. She slammed the door in his face and tried to lock it, but she was too late. He slipped through the crack, threw the door open, and had her trapped.

What happened next happened fast, but for Molly it seemed like everything was in slow motion.

A large, round hay bale in the loft above and behind Roland started to move. It rocked back and forth, and then it fell—or was pushed, rather—and fell straight on him, knocking him out cold.

When Molly looked up she saw the girl—Ashley—standing in the loft looking down at her with a satis-fied smile.

When Sheriff Starbuck and his deputies came out to arrest Roland, she found it hard to explain how *she* got the huge bale to budge and roll over on the soon-to-be-ex-mayor.

"I guess it's just super-human strength that kicks in when you're in a panic," she explained, knowing she'd never tell anyone what really happened. She knew they would never believe her.

But *I* believe her. You see, I *am* Ashley.

Epilogue

El Dorado Springs will never be a booming metropolis. Nor do we want it to be. All we want is for Main Street to be like the good ol' days with busy store fronts and patrons having to circle around the park at least once to find an open parking space.

The revitalization committee is still working round the clock trying to bring in new businesses. Wilhelmina and Katherine are in the process of concocting a statewide advertising campaign to lure would-be business owners to our area with the promise of grant money left by Ollie.

While Roland Thurman sits in the state penitentiary in Northern Missouri, Councilman Brad True is acting mayor until a new one is elected. He's getting ready to sign the ordinance proposed by Wilhelmina and the revitalization committee to keep Bobby Joe Allen from painting Spring Street Tavern in Kansas City Chiefs colors—or any other colors not pre-approved by the committee, for that matter.

The Allison boys just painted the Old Opry House a tasteful pink and beige—but not before graciously seeking approval from the committee.

Foundation 81—a new store on the corner of Spring and Main Streets—just opened a few weeks ago. They've got just about everything: shoes, clothes, jewelry, household items, even a soda fountain in the back.

Allison Shinkle rented the building across from the El Dorado Springs Sun and runs a flower shop: Allie's Floral Creations and Gifts.

Rumor has it that a few other businesses—a shoe store and a thrift shop—are opening later in the fall.

Jennifer and Molly have patched things up, but regardless of how many "talking-tos" Molly gives her, Jennifer still hasn't broken things off with Winthrop. Every time she's tried he'll buy her a sparkly, expensive trinket that will change her mind. He still promises to divorce Constance, although he hasn't bothered to let Constance know.

Speaking of Constance, she still pines for Michael, but he's too busy pining for Peggy—I mean *Summer Stevens*—when he's not trying to run a newspaper, be the lead reporter, and raise a pre-teen daughter.

Anne-Donavan still runs KESM while her good-for-nothing brother spends money as fast as it comes in.

Jerry Ray Turner and Kathryn McCarty still keep folks 'round here entertained with their glitz and glamour.

Speaking of "glitz and glamour," our girl Sydney Friar will be headed off to Las Vegas soon to compete in the Miss America Pageant.

As for me? Well, Mama always said I was special and really good at helping people. She said I'd always be a part of this town, and it looks like she was right, although I know this isn't exactly what she had in mind.

But being a Guardian Angel definitely has its privileges. I get to watch out, not just for Molly, but this town I loved my whole life. I still get to be a part of it and be privy to everything from the past. And while I can't predict or see the future, I get to stay here and watch it unfold.

And of course I can't forget The Hillbilly Debutante Café, still the hottest spot in town. A special booth was recently dedicated to Ollie Green, and the past two weeks folks have been debating the hotly contested mayoral campaign between none other than Winthrop Worthington and Michael Dailey.

So, things are looking up for our little city. We no longer look like a ghost town, but we do still have a ways to go to be restored to our full glory and splendor. It will happen. I'm sure of it.

But you know, I'm not even worried about it anyway. This town isn't going anywhere. How do I know? Because it's like I told you in the beginning: at the end of the day, the most important thing about El Dorado Springs, Missouri, isn't the park or the spring water; it's the people. And no matter how far away we may get, we always ended up trying to get back here just as fast as we can.